Chasing Charlie Chan

Dave Crosby

PublishAmerica
Baltimore

ISBN: 1-4241-7251-9
PUBLISHED BY PUBLISHAMERICA, LLLP
www.publishamerica.com
Baltimore

To Mary C. Crosby—my mom.

There it was, on the official promotion list. Chandler, Charlie NMI from Uniformed Officer Grade 7 to Detective, Homicide.

Police Headquarters – Campbell, Ohio – Friday, 6/18 – 0800 hrs.

"Spencer!"

John Spencer is jolted out of his daydream. With a slight sigh he sinks back into his chair. He knows the Chief will scream again.

"Spencer, get in here!"

John's desk is just outside Chief of Police George Fadler's glass enclosed cubical. He hates the arrangement—no privacy at all. The boss can see who's visiting or even if John is there. He isn't sure if Fadler can hear his conversations, but he feels like his every move is under a microscope...and it is. Fadler is that kind of boss.

Typically, that desk would be occupied by a secretary, but the department did away with private secretaries some years ago. John doesn't like being so close to the boss. However, Chief Fadler has less than six months to go to retirement, and since John is senior man...well, John is slated to be the next Chief of Police. He can put up with the arrangement for a few more months. Being the heir-apparent is not without problems.

"Spencer. You out there?"

John knows he has used all the delay time possible, so he hurries into the chief's office. In the past, the chief had asked him to bring a stenographer's pad when called but John used his last bit of courage to fight that. He didn't want to take on the secretary's role or image. The secretary desk thing was bad enough.

He often wonders what visitors must think when they see the seating arrangement. To be safe, he carries a half dozen three by five cards in his back pocket. He might want to take notes someday. The cards are really unnecessary since Fadler never has a great thought. He just barks orders—take care of this, take care of that.

John Spencer stands in front of Chief Fadler's desk, but the chief doesn't look up. He continues to pour over the computer tab run in front of him. He chomps his cigar, curses under his breath, and bangs his fat hand on the desk.

John thinks of how much Fadler reminds him of a giant toad.

"Who the hell's responsible for this crap?" Fadler yells, without looking up.

"What crap is that, sir?"

Fadler looks up at John through a cloud of cigar smoke. He brings his palm down hard on the pile of paper again.

"This crap." Pounding, pounding, pounding. "This promotion list crap. There's gotta be a mistake here someplace. Big time! I can't believe it. Have you checked this out?"

John waves the cigar smoke aside. Bracing his legs on the edge of the desk, he leans forward to get a closer look at the paper in front of his boss. He cocks his head as far as it will go, but still can't see what has Fadler so upset.

"What's the problem, sir?"

"What's the problem? What's the problem? You don't see it? How the hell are you going to run this department when I'm not here to hold your hand? I'm out of here. I've only got 169 days to go, you know."

"One sixty eight, sir."

"Whatever."

John stands silent like the ex-marine he is. That's all he can do.

He knows that the chief will get to the point soon.

Chief George Fadler was a clean-desk man. There was never more than one piece of paper on his desk at any time. A telephone, a gigantic ashtray, and a neat row of finely sharpened 2B pencils. Oh yes, and a pink eraser; that's it. To some, he appears to be mean, but in reality, he's more stupid than mean. He is taken to saying stupid things that turn out to be mean. He operates from a position of fear; so he questions every action of his subordinates, and disagrees with most of their conclusions. He reached his level of incompetence long ago, and deep down inside, he knows it. He got this job by hanging on and by kissing every ass higher than his own.

Looking up at John, with an expression as sour as he could possibly make it, he brings his palm down hard on the paper again. John flinches. "Here, right here! Charlie Chandler promoted to Detective! Charlie Chandler! A woman! Good God!"

"You think it's a mistake, sir? She had to qualify, and pass the exam. That detective exam is murder. I had a very hard time with it." Inside, John is laughing at the fact that Fadler would not be able to pass the exam.

"Mistake? Mistake? Good God, man, having a broad on the police force is a mistake! Now she's a detective!"

John cringes; he moves his lips and bobs his head slightly to mimic the chief's words. He's heard this rant a least a hundred times.

"I was on the force before women and dogs!"

"And blacks, sir?" John added.

"Yeah, them too!"

Ignoring John, the chief goes back to his mumbling and cigar-chomping as he continues to study the pages as if it was the first time he had seen it.

Because he was so short, he had to keep his chair close to his desk. Because he was so fat, his chest touched the edge of the desk, and he seemed to hunch over his work.

John knows the rant is over. He hurries back to his desk and plops into his chair. Sessions with Fadler are always exhausting. He pulls out the typewriter tray and examines the large calendar he has taped there. He slips his pen from his shirt pocket, and with a slight smile places a large X on today's date.

"One sixty-eight to go, I was right," he says to himself.

John has worked hard to get as far as he has. He didn't start out with the Campbell police force, but joined when he decided to move from Columbus to a small town. He has never been married, so he's never bought a house. However, as taxes increased, so did his rent. Anyway, he was tired of hearing his landlord complain about the cost of things, when it was John paying the bill.

Being an outstanding police officer, he advanced to Assistant Chief in six years. He's well respected by all the police officer, and always willing to help anyone in trouble.

7

At an even six feet, one hundred eighty-five pounds, John is in very good shape for a forty-year-old bachelor. Many of his friends drink and smoke, but John never developed either habit. It's not that he didn't try. He lit up a cigarette when he was about twelve, but got so dizzy that it scared him away from cigarettes forever. He even tried chewing tobacco once while he was camping with the Boy Scouts. One of the boys had a plug of Red Man chewing tobacco. They cut the little bar into small squares, and each boy took one to chew. It smelled sweet, but John never got past the second bite before he lost his dinner. Most of the other boys joined him. As for alcohol, he just couldn't get past the smell. So, for those reasons, John probably extended his life span by twenty years or so.

He's single, but dates three different women. Nothing serious, just good friends. He enjoys being with them. The idea of marriage has him terrified.

John rocks back in his chair and swings his feet up on the typewriter tray. He clamps his hands behind his neck and tries to restart the daydream he was working on before Fadler called him.

Fadler's office occupies the corner of a huge room known as the pit. Its wall-to-wall cops. A row of desks along each wall, and two rows of facing desks down the middle. The room wasn't planned for this setup, so telephone and electrical wires hang from the ceiling. The back-to-back desks share a computer mounted on a gadget that lets it swing from one desk to the other. The walls are painted green and white. A band of green, about four feet high, runs up from the floor, and then it's painted white to the top of the wall. Portraits of past police chiefs hang along the back wall.

Like any busy office full of people, there is the hum of conversation and equipment. The noise and movement in the big room, as people work, fade in John's mind. He can see his imaginary dream-boat—a thirty-five-foot catamaran—cutting through the waves of Lake Erie. John's at the helm. What should he name her? He needed something clever like the rest of the boats at his imaginary boat club. Before he can decide, the all too familiar alarm sounds again.

"Spencer!"

Jolted from his dream, John immediately stands at attention. He shakes his head as if trying to shake off a deep sleep.

"Spencer! You out there?"

John answers the call like the trooper his is.

"Yes, sir?"

"Where is this Chandler broad now?"

"Her desk is downstairs, sir. I was thinking of moving her up here tomorrow."

"Save your time. Leave the stupid broad where she is."

"Oh, she's not stupid, sir; far from it. In fact, I think she's a genius. She has a high I.Q.—belongs to that genius club. Nice looking too."

"Can she cook, and clean the place up?" says Fadler, and gives that remark a real belly laugh.

John rolls his eyes. "I don't think so, sir. She *is* a police officer, and a detective, sir."

Fadler shakes his head, as if he's feeling sorry for himself. "All I need is some broad whining about everything."

John steps up to the desk. "Oh, I don't think she'll whine, sir. She was a marine. She can take care of herself. Marines don't whine, sir. She has a great record as a uniformed cop."

John holds up a thick file folder.

"Do you want to see her personnel file?"

Fadler shakes his head in disgust.

"A lady marine?"

"A drill instructor, sir; combat, lots of ribbons."

"Drill instructor? She probably has a foul mouth. I can't stand a woman who swears."

"She doesn't swear, sir. She wouldn't say shit if she had both hands full."

"How do you know so much about this broad?"

"Personnel file, plus she goes to the same church I do."

"Good God! A religious wacko!"

John gives up and just stands there. His shoulders sink waiting for the next barrage. It's obvious that Fadler doesn't know one of his most outstanding police officers.

"Let's put your nice looking, brainy, church going jarhead broad to work. Get her up here so I can *welcome* her to the department." He chuckled at his little "welcome" joke.

John lets all that pass. "She's out on her beat now. Her shift ends…" John checks his watch, "…in about two hours. I'll have her report up here when she checks in."

Fadler doesn't look up; he just dismisses John with a wave of the back of his hand. John is glad to leave. He walks down the long hall to the communications center. It only takes a second to write out a short message: "Report to Chief Fadler's Office at the end of your shift. Spencer." He hands the note to the dispatcher who acknowledges with a nod. The message goes out and Charlie gives it a 10-4.

Officer Charlie Chandler is about to begin a new phase of her life. She's always wanted to be a detective and now she is one. There's an old adage that says, "Be careful what you wish for, you might get it."

On Duty With Charlie Chandler – Friday, 6/18 – 1432 hrs.

Charlie Chandler drives her Ford cruiser at high speed in pursuit of a car-jacked Lexus sedan. She calls for backup and settles in for a long chase. It happens this way. This is dangerous, she knows that she must stay focused. Charlie always follows department procedure to the letter. She lives in fear that she will do something wrong and stain her father's reputation.

She knows that this guy can't keep going forever, unless of course the Lexus is equipped with an atomic engine. If she plays by the rules, she'll get him, and nobody will get hurt.

She gets a cold chill. *Gas!* she thinks. *Do I have enough gas?* She looks down at the gage. Three quarters full. No problem.

Much to Charlie's surprise, the Lexus slows down and pulls over. She half expects the driver to jump out and make a run for it, but the door remains closed. This is a bad sign; it could mean trouble. Charlie calls in the action on her shoulder mike and requests backup again. She swings her cruiser into position, by the book, of course; everything by the book. Slowly, she opens the door and slides out, slipping her gun from its holster. Resting her forearms on the top of the open door and with both hands on the weapon, she tries to get a good look at the driver. She can see a shape bobbing around in the front seat. She yells, "Driver...put your hands out the window!" The window glides down, but no hands come out. Loud music with a heavy beat does.

Louder, "Driver, put your hands out the window!"

One hand appears. A left hand.

"Both hands! Put both hands out. Now!" screams Charlie.

Another hand appears.

Charlie moves from behind the door and steps a little closer. "Driver. Step out of the car." The door opens and a young man climbs out. He has a smirk on his face.

Starting when she was a kid, Charlie developed the habit of describing people in her mind so that she could be a good witness. How could she be a good cop if she couldn't describe people?

She actually describes the man—what she was seeing—to herself—out loud, but in a very low voice. "White, maybe 25-28, at lease six feet tall, dark complection, short black hair, tiny beard under his lower lip, black pants, Bears football jersey, tattoos galore, Nike running shoes, Yankee's ball cap. Smart-ass smirk." She puts that all in her memory bank along with hundreds of others.

The guy turns to face Charlie. Charlie yells, "Turn around, face away from me! Walk backward toward the sound of my voice."

Nothing happens; the guy just stands there, head bobbing to the beat coming from the car. Charlie starts to burn. She grinds her teeth then yells again. This time she puts an emphasis on each word. Each word is its own sentence. "Put. Your. Hands. On. Top. Of. Your. Head. And. MOVE!"

The guy takes off his ball cap, and tosses it into the car. Then he clasps his hands on the back of his neck.

"On TOP of your head, stupid."

The driver complies and starts to walk backward toward Charlie. She yells, "Stop!" when he gets close enough. Cautiously she steps forward and grabs his thumbs. She holsters her piece, and makes a quick pat down. No gun. Still holding the guy, she glances around to see if backup has arrived; it hasn't. She pulls one of the guy's arms down to clip on a handcuff. Before she can even get one bracelet closed, he spins and delivers an elbow to the side of Charlie's head. She staggers—he runs.

Charlie shakes her head and starts running in pursuit. He's fast, but she's faster. She gets close enough to get both hands on the guy's shoulders and uses her weight to bring him down…hard. She climbs up his frame and plants a knee firmly on the back of his neck, pressing his face firmly to the ground. He moans. He wiggles, and the knee presses harder. He relaxes. She's burning mad, and anything but gentle. Arms get jerked around, and cuffs go on. She staggers to her feet and starts brushing herself off. Standing over the guy, she struggles to catch her breath.

Backup arrives. "About time," she mumbles as she reaches down and takes hold of the handcuffs.

She jerks the guy to his feet. He screams and yells, "I didn't do nothin'!"

Holding his arms just short of ripping them off, Charlie delivers the guy to the two uniformed officers waiting by their black and white. As Charlie drags the driver along, one officer calls out, "Hey, Charlie, congrats on your promotion. Good job."

"You guys handle this? The Lexus is hot, he hijacked it. I don't know if anyone was hurt. Better check. Nobody inside. I didn't do a search. Check the Yankee's cap. I'll bet it has a little surprise inside for you."

She moves up close to the prisoner. Standing on her toes—up close in the guy's face—she yells in her best drill instructor voice, "You can add resisting arrest, assaulting a police officer, and every driving violation you can think of!" She steps away, brushes some more.

Charlie checks her watch. "I gotta go…command performance with Fadler."

She turns and runs to her car. With a long screech of the tires, the cruiser speeds off. The two cops and the bad guy watch in awe.

One cop jerks on the guy's cuffs. "You got mixed up with the wrong lady, buddy."

Fadler's Office – Friday, 6/18 – 1623 hrs.

With John leading the way, Charlie walks into Fadler's office and takes her place alongside him, in front of the chief's desk. They both stand at attention...once a marine, always a marine.

Fadler slowly looks up, but avoids Charlie's eyes.

"Your uniform is a disgrace, lady," barks Fadler.

Charlie checks herself out. Her shirt has a small rip under her arm, and the elbow has a large hole that shows a skinned-up and bloody elbow. Her trousers don't look too much better. No holes, but plenty of dirt. Her left cheek is red from her on-the-job struggle.

"Yes, sir, I had a little action with a bad guy on the way over. You know how it is."

Fadler wants to get it over with. "Okay, report to work in civvies Monday morning. Keep in mind that you're on thirty-day probation. Screw up and you're back on the street." Without another word, he gets up and waddles out the door.

John and Charlie exchange puzzled glances.

"Is that it?" says Charlie

"Welcome aboard," replies John.

Her promotion to detective shouldn't be a surprise. Anyone who knows Charlie knows she deserves it. Charlie had advanced fast because of solid achievements in police work on her part. She started out like every other cop. After graduation from the academy, she worked as a lowly patrol officer, driving a black and white.

Call it luck, or call it skill, or call it instinct, but when Charlie spotted the rental van headed east on Main Street the hair went up on the back of her neck. The van wasn't speeding or weaving, or even changing lanes. Charlie noticed the left turn signal was blinking, but it passed intersection after intersection without turning. She hit the lights and siren. The van pulled over and the rest is history, as they say.

It turned out to be the biggest drug bust since year one. Biggest ever! The van was jam-packed full of neat packages of cocaine. The newspapers reported that it had a street value of over four hundred million dollars!

Charlie received a promotion, a commendation, a medal, plus a write-up in *Time* magazine. She became the darling of her political bosses who trotted her out every election year, to show what *they* had done to eliminate drugs. Charlie is painfully shy. She hated all the attention. Somehow, her direct-line boss, Fadler, never heard of her.

How can she convince Fadler that she can do the job?

Charlie's House – Friday, 6/18 – 1930 hrs.

Charlie sits at the kitchen table. Leaning on one elbow, her hand holds up a long face. She's not eating, just poking at her dinner with her fork.

Her mother stands by the stove, spatula in hand, finishing up the meal. "Having a problem, honey?"

"I guess so," moans Charlie.

"Let's talk," says Mom.

Mom sets the spatula aside and takes a seat at the table. She wipes her hands on her apron, looks at Charlie, and waits.

Charlie and her Mom are best friends. They enjoy each other's company and share the good and the bad as it comes along. They live in the house where Charlie was born twenty-eight years ago. It's your typical two-story small town frame house. A small lot with a tiny garage in the back, facing the alley. The garage was built when cars were much smaller so Charlie needs a compact car to use it. Her Volkswagen Beetle fits in nicely. Except for the color, the house is just like most of the houses on Elm Street. Charlie loves this old house and knows that someday, when she finds Mister Right, she will raise her kids here.

"Job got you down, baby?" Mom asks.

"You know, Mom, I don't know why, but I think it has. I'm a full-fledged detective now. I've spent years getting ready for this job, so

I know I can handle it." Charlie is lying to her Mom and to herself. Her stomach is churning; she's worried sick. "It will be great fun! I'm just a little nervous."

"What's eating at you?"

"I'm not too thrilled with my boss. Fadler—he's the chief—let me know that if I screw up, I'm out. Not a nice way to start out on a new job."

She pauses and looks at the ceiling to think. "I sure didn't get off on the right foot today. I don't think the chief likes me. Maybe I should have changed my uniform before I went in there."

Mom reaches across the table and puts her hand on Charlie's. "Oh, you can handle it alright. You've been in training for this job your whole life. Your dad saw to that. You were born a cop. Let's drive up to Columbus and spend the weekend shopping. We can celebrate your promotion, and relax a little. I want to see that new show at the State, and we can have lunch at the new place on High Street."

Charlie Chandler is a cop. Her father was a cop; her grandfather was a cop. It's all she ever wanted to be. Get the bad guys. Truth, Justice, and the American way, like Superman. She wasn't a tomboy, but as a little girl she played cops and robbers with the boys, and left the dolls to the other girls. She has read every mystery story she could find. Charlie and her dad loved the old Charlie Chan movies. They watched every one of them…over, and over, and over. It drove Mom nuts. Charlie knows most of the old Charlie Chan sayings by heart, and she uses them when they apply.

Mom leaves the table. When she returns, she hands Charlie a gold medallion about the size of a silver dollar hanging from a heavy gold chain. "It was your dad's. He wore it all the time; claimed it brought him luck. He got it in China. He went over there in the sixties on some kind of program to train, or get trained. I forget. He brought that token back with him."

Charlie is thrilled. She wants more than anything to be like her father, a clever and successful detective. Inside, she's full of doubt. How could she possibly be as good a detective as Dad? She studies the disk. It's covered with Chinese figures. Three large characters in the center, and a bunch of little characters around the edge.

15

"What does it say?"

"Are you kidding?"

"Did Dad know?"

"He pretended to, but would never tell me. He liked to string me along."

Charlie pulls the chain over her head. She holds the medallion in her fingers, and strokes it with her thumb. A big smile. "Wow, it makes me feel close to him." She looks down at the medallion and smiles a very soft smile. "I miss him so much."

Mom wipes a tear from her cheek.

Charlie picks up her fork and takes a deep breath. She's all smiles. "Let's eat! Tomorrow's a busy day—shop till we drop!"

Deep down inside, she's still worried and afraid.

Charlie's House – Monday, 6/21 – 0515 hrs.

Charlie and Mom spent the weekend in Columbus shopping. They had a wonderful time, but Charlie can't shake her feeling about starting her new job.

The alarm clock screams, but Charlie doesn't move. She's been awake for hours, worrying. A lazy arm flops over and turns the thing off.

She swings her legs over, sits up on the edge of the bed, and tries to shake the cotton out of her head. For the next five minutes, she just sits. Nothing's working, including her brain.

With a "Ho Hum" she staggers to the bathroom.

The hot shower makes her feel like going back to bed, but she dismisses that from her mind. She tries singing. She remembers a rule from Dad's Dale Carnegie course: "If you act enthusiastic, you will feel enthusiastic." She starts repeating that mantra and bouncing a little while she brushes her teeth. She's coming alive.

"If you act enthusiastic, you will feel enthusiastic," she chants as she dances around, getting dressed. Suddenly, she gets an idea.

Charlie runs to the bookshelf and searches. She grabs three books: *The Seven Habits of Successful Detectives, Strictly Murder,* and

Crime Scene Investigation. She piles the books up on her arm and walks to the small desk which she hardly ever uses. The desk is covered with just about everything. It's the place where things end up when there's no specific place for them. The books join the pile.

In a cluttered drawer, she find a stack of 3 X 5 cards and takes out a few. The rest go back in the drawer and she pushes it closed. She pulls the chair around to the desk, but when she sits down, there's no place to work; the desk top is too crowded. Panic stricken, she plops the books on her bed, sits down and grabs the closest one. With a pencil clamped crosswise in her teeth, she starts searching through it. "Here's something," she mumbles. Out comes the pencil and on one card she writes, *The Five W's*. Below that she lists, *Who, What, Why, When, Where and How*. Under that she writes the rule: *Never ask a question that can be answered Yes or No*. Pencil back in her mouth, she searches again. More mumbling…another card. On this one, she writes a title and underlines it, *Questions*, and lists them.

How long did you know _____ ?
How much money did _____ owe you?
What kind of drugs did _____ use?
Did _____ prefer boys or girls?
Who did _____ hang out with? Any suspicious characters?
Who did _____ fire recently?
Which secret societies did _____ belong to?
How did _____ get along with people?
What has been _____ mental state?
Who were _____ enemies?

She walks to her closet and tucks the cards in the pocket of her new suit, then starts to put the books on the book shelf, then just dumps them on the desk.

A line from her favorite Broadway musical, *Fiddler on the Roof,* comes to mind. In the play, Tevya, the poor milkman, sings, "When you're rich, they think you really know." She chuckles. "Maybe if I act like I know, people will think that I really do," she mumbles.

Charlie appears in the kitchen wearing the new suit that she bought to start her new job. Inside her head, she chants the Dale Carnegie mantra. *If you act enthusiastic, you'll feel enthusiastic.* It works. It's a conservative business suit, but leaves little doubt that she's a woman, even with room for her gun. It's just right for a lady detective. She spins around so Mom can see.

"Charlie, you're gorgeous," says Mom.

Charlie is gorgeous. She's today's woman, tall, slim, self-confident. She wears her hair short, in what they used to call a pixie cut, or Peter Pan. She got tired of having to tuck long hair under her police hat. Her hair is a naturally deep red or auburn, and she has just enough freckles to give her a Huck Finn appearance. Charlie is anything but a boy. She has the grace of the woman she is.

Charlie couldn't have felt better. "You know, Mom, there's something about putting on new clothes. It makes you feel clean and special."

"It sure does, Charlie, I know exactly what you mean."

Charlie digs into her breakfast. Mom fiddles around the stove.

"You know what, Mom?"

Mom shrugs her shoulders, and turns her palms up. She has a flash of memory of Charlie saying those exact words hundreds and hundreds of times when she was a little girl.

"No. What, Charlie?" Mom answers, like always.

"I had this crazy dream last night. It was so real! I dreamed that Charlie Chan came to teach me all his methods so I could be a successful detective. Maybe Charlie Chan is going to help me."

Mom shakes her head slowly. "You're as bad as your father. Charlie Chan was a movie character; a fictional character. He wasn't real, Charlie. He wasn't real."

Charlie smiled. "I know that, Mom. But the ideas are real. The methods are just great. Plus, he spouted Chinese wisdom. Charlie Chan had a saying for every occasion. That was great. Dad and I talked about it all the time."

"Yes, and they used to call him Charlie Chan."

"That wouldn't be so bad."

"No. Actually, I think he liked it. He was the best detective this town ever had. Better than they deserved."

Charlie has a feeling of doubt creeping in, but shakes it off. She holds up her medallion and strokes it with her thumb.

"It's a good day, Mom."

Inside her head, the little voice reminds her to give it her all; for Dad.

Mom smiled. "It's a good day, Charlie. You want more toast?"

Suddenly, a tune starts playing in Charlie's head, and she whistles. "Hi ho, hi ho, it's off to work we go…" She's feeling better.

Fadler's Office – Monday, 6/21 – 0800 hrs.

Charlie appears outside Fadler's door at eight A.M. sharp. When John sees her he jumps up and motions her to the open door. He notices the new suit and thinks how sharp she looks. "You look nice. He's waiting." Charlie smiles…that felt good.

Like two good marines, they march to the boss' desk…in step, of course.

Fadler doesn't move. Charlie checks out the office. The wall behind Fadler is almost blank. Every other office she's been in has the walls covered with photos, awards, and plaques. Fadler's wall has an eight by ten black and white photo, and a very small plaque shaped like a shield. She can't read the plaque, or identify anyone in the photo.

Slowly, Fadler looks up.

"Well, you're right on time. Good, I like that. It's your lucky day."

"Yes, sir! I'm glad to be here," Charlie bubbles.

"Whatever…A call just came in from that carnival freak show out on Walnut Creek. Somebody got whacked, and you're the only one I can spare to handle it."

Spare? It was like getting hit in the chest. Charlie ponders, *I get a murder case on my first day? That gives me 29 days to catch the bad guy. Now he tells me that I'm all he can spare.*

John didn't pick up on the "freak" comment. "We don't say 'freak' any longer, sir."

"We, who? You got a mouse in your pocket?" Fadler chuckles at his little joke. He'd used that line at least a hundred times before.

19

"It's a carnival—with a side show, sir. They are performers."

Fadler takes a big draw on his cigar, lets it out, and watches the smoke curl up in front of him.

As if Charlie isn't there, Fadler says, "The perfect case for a brainy broad. Maybe she'll find out that police work is more than taking some damn test."

Charlie's eyebrows flash. *That hurt. Is this the way it's going to be? Brainy broad?*

Fadler looks at Charlie and waves his hand toward the door. "Well…Go!"

Charlie is shocked, but keeps her cool. "Yes, sir!" she snaps.

John shakes his head every so slightly. He knows that he has lost this battle.

"I'll get on it right away, sir. I'll put detective Chandler on that case right away."

It's all like a dream to Charlie. She's there but somehow she isn't. She's watching from above. *Is this what they mean by an out-of-body experience?* she thinks. *Am I having an out-of-body experience?*

Charlie speaks up. "Oh, what will I do about a car, sir?"

Where did that come from? Did I say that? she wonders.

As if in pain, Fadler reaches into a large desk drawer and pull out a giant red warning light, about ten inches tall and eight inches wide; the type they plug into the cigarette lighter and put on top of an unmarked car. He shoves it across the desk, like he's glad to get rid of it.

"Here. Use your car. I think you get twenty-five or thirty cents a mile, or something."

Charlie reluctantly picks up the light and looks it over. *Thirty cents a mile to use a brand new Volkswagen Bug?* It's obvious that she's not pleased with the idea of using her brand new little yellow baby for police work.

"What about a partner, sir? Have you assigned someone to be my partner?"

Fadler puffs. "Oh yeah…partner…I'll take care of it…you better head out for Walnut Creek." With a smug smile he adds, "That body's getting cold…or should I say colder?"

Charlie makes a marine-style right-face, and marches out of the office. She is shaken. John stays behind.

Chief Fadler closes his beady little eyes into slits, and holds up his index finger pointing straight up.

"Wait a minute. Hold it…hold it…hold it!" Talking to himself.

John turns and stands. He knows this routine. His boss has had a great thought and will soon lay it on him.

"Sir?"

"Chandler. Charlie Chandler. I knew that name was familiar. We had a guy named Charlie Chandler on the force years ago. Charlie Chandler. We called him Charlie Chan. Is that his kid? Old Charlie Chan is back. Back as a woman," he chuckles.

The chief actually giggles as if he had solved a great puzzle. He's proud of himself.

John jumps at the chance to impress his boss.

"That was Charlie's father. He was a cop. Her grandfather was a cop too."

Fadler's face sours. "I didn't know the old guy, but I knew Charlie Chan all right. Never liked the guy. He was promoted to Inspector. All politics; luck and politics."

By this time, John is at the door.

"Anything else, sir?"

"Yeah, call personnel and have them transfer that kid in Traffic over here to be Chandler's partner. He's been bugging me for a year now."

"Will do," says John.

Fadler slowly shakes his head and swings his chair back where it belongs. John knows that his boss is hatching some kind of scheme. He doesn't ask about it; he walks out.

21

Walnut Creek Amusement Park – Monday, 6/21 – 0845 hrs.

The yellow Volkswagen pulls up to the main gate of the Walnut Creek amusement park—red light flashing. Charlie stops at the small dilapidated guard shack, and waits for something to happen. Her first impression is that a coat of paint wouldn't even start to help this place.

"Damn!" She looks around for some sign of life inside the guard shack. Nothing happens.

"No sirens," she says to herself, and she leans hard on the horn.

The door on the guard shack slowly creaks open and a very old, very wrinkled man, in a very old, very wrinkled uniform staggers out the door. He looks down at Charlie.

"You can't come in here, lady. We don't open till noon."

"Police!" yells Charlie. She holds up her badge.

"Noon," says the guard.

"Who's in charge of this outfit?"

"You can come in when we open at noon. Come back then." The guard turns and walks back into the shack and the door closes.

"Boy," mumbles Charles, "I sure impressed the hell outa him."

With that, she slams her foot down on the gas peddle and heads into the park, red light flashing. She stops at the top of a crest that gives her a panoramic view of the whole park. She jerks on the wire to unplug the red light.

Walnut Creek amusement park was built in the early forties, just prior to World War Two. It wasn't actually built as a carnival and freak show; it was just a large field—maybe two football fields—where a traveling carnival could set up. A polluted creek, Walnut Creek, runs along the back edge of the property. It was polluted fifty hears ago, but nobody cares.

Near the end of the great depression, the last carnival to arrive ran out of money and stayed. The property in those days wasn't worth anything, so staying solved most of their problems. It became Walnut Creek Amusement Park. Disney World North, it's not.

Charlie steps out of her bug and looks around. No people. *It's hot*, she thinks. Mumbling to herself she says, "It's only June and it's already so hot." She opens her coat and looks down. "This suit is not going to fly. I've got to come up with something more comfortable...maybe I better switch back to my uniform."

A large frame building houses a restaurant; the small structure next to it hides the public rest rooms. She cringes at the thought of what the rest rooms must be like.

The restaurant has a large metal electric sign over the door. It measures at least three by five feet, painted bright red. The boarder is a wide yellow stripe with golf-ball-size light bulbs that blink in order to simulate movement all the way around. In the middle are three large letters painted in yellow and filled with regular size light bulbs. They blink "EAT."

Charlie smiles at the sign. *Advertising at its best*, she thinks.

About fifty feet from the restaurant is a huge tent-like structure that holds the side show. As Charlie will learn, it's called the Show Tent. It's actually a gigantic tent covering a frame building where the performers live and work. Giant canvas posters hang all along the outside wall. A five-foot-wide stage runs the length of the front— maybe four feet off the ground. The posters are all hand-painted in bright colors. The subjects of the posters—the performers—are not very realistic, but somehow it makes them more interesting. Charlie can't help but think these would be worth a bundle in today's antique market.

Just outside the double-flap entranceway is a podium and an incredibly small ticket booth. The two-dollar price of admission is painted in big letters on the front. The booth is red, trimmed and decorated in yellow. Standing at just the right angle, Charlie can see where various prices have been over-painted many times. The words "Freak Show" faintly shows through on one side.

The inside is a large dirt floor arena, with a horseshoe-shaped stage that runs around the sides and back. The entrance is the open end of the horseshoe. Unseen to visitors, behind the poster are small apartments for the performers.

Nearby, under a large spreading oak tree sits an old-time circus wagon. *It's beautiful*, she thinks. It's highly decorated in bright colors and fancy decorations. It's one of those things you would like to own, but would have nothing to do with it. It belongs right where it is. The wagon is about thirty feet long and eight feet wide. The bottom is maybe four feet off the ground. A set of wooded stairs at the end gives access to the Dutch door. Charlie can't help looking at the wheels. They are very large, almost as tall as she is, and wonderfully decorated. Somebody put a lot of tender loving care into this thing. She considers how great it would be to have one of these wheels in the living room.

The rest of the park holds a collection of typical carnival rides. They all look like they are being held together with hundreds and hundreds of layers of paint. A small Ferris wheel dominates the scene. A long building, labeled "Fun House," serves as the backdrop to the park. It too is covered with brightly painted cartoons showing women with their skirts being blown up, and strange characters laughing hysterically.

Charlie scans the place looking for life. She spots a couple of white vans near the trees on the far edge of the park, by the creek. "Crime scene people, I'll bet," she mumbles. She climbs in the Volkswagen, plugs in the red light, and heads for the white vans.

Charlie was right. The crime scene investigators are on the job. When they see the yellow Volkswagen their first impulse is to stop it from entering the crime scene, but the flashing red light means police. It's okay.

Charlie pulls up close to the yellow tape and shuts down the car. She unplugs the red light, pulls it down from the roof, and tosses it on the passenger's seat. Before she gets out, she fishes out her badge and put the holder in her breast pocket with the badge hanging out.

The leader of the investigators approaches Charlie with an inquisitive look. Charlie puts out her hand. "Detective Chandler," she says. Inside, Charlie smiles at the sound of the word detective. This is the first time that she's used the term—in public.

"Wilson," says the man, "Jeremiah Wilson…C.S. Unit. You got this case?"

Charlie nods. "I'm the lucky one. What happened?"

"You can call me Jerry if you like. The owner of this flea circus got whacked on the head and decided it was best to go ahead and croak."

Jeremiah Wilson is about forty years old, five ten or eleven, one eighty pounds, black, balding. He has a tiny, thin mustache, and wears horn-rim glasses. He's dressed in blue jeans, t-shirt and running shoes. A ball cap is folded and tucked into his back pocket. Pleasant man, nice voice.

Charlie offers a weak smile at the joke. She wonders how Jeremiah could possibly trim that mustache. One slip of the razor and it's gone. He sure doesn't dress like they do on CSI Miami.

"Are you guys about done?"

"We need another half hour or so; we need a few more pictures. You can look at the body if you want."

Charlie ducks under the yellow tape and follows Wilson to the edge of the creek, where a man is stretched out. He's face down, and the gash in the back of his head is easy to see. In fact, the back of his head is almost gone!

"Wow," says Charlie, "somebody didn't like him."

"You got it."

Charlie squats down to get a closer look. "What's the TOD?"

"I'd say about five or six hours ago, but you'll have to wait till the Medical Examiner takes a peek. Five or six hours, that's my guess, anyway."

Charlie looks at her watch and counts backward. "About two—three a.m.?"

He nods.

"Does the media know yet?" asks Charlie.

"I haven't said anything to anybody. I've got more than enough to keep me busy without that bunch. Anyway, they have a trained vulture that circles around until it spots a body, and the bird calls in. They'll show up. You can count on it."

Charlie grins. *God, I hope I don't have to do one of those TV interviews with people yelling at you and sticking a microphone in your face.*

Charlie watches as Wilson squirts blood from a syringe into a gadget hooked up to a laptop computer. He pokes a few keys and steps back and looks at the screen.

"What's that gadget?" asks Charlie.

"Well, it's new, and we're just starting to use it. It's a wireless laptop with this thing plugged in. It transmits stuff back to the office and we can get a blood analysis right here. Right at the crime scene, can you imagine? I can even I.D. prints using that little scanner in my case."

"DNA?" asks Charlie.

Wilson smiles and shakes his head. "It's not quite that sophisticated, but in about two minutes I'll know if there were any drugs or booze involved. In fact, it will tell me which drugs were found." He chuckles. "But not which brand of booze."

Charlie is impressed, but can only muster up a faint, "Wow."

"Oh yeah," says Charlie, "can you loan me a couple of DNA swabs?"

"Don't you carry some in your car?"

"My regular cruiser is in the shop," she lies. "I had to use my car."

Wilson checks his case, and digs out a handful of DNA tubes with the swabs inside. He hands them to Charlie.

"Make sure you label them while you're still looking at the person. That's standard procedure. You can't imagine how many times DNA samples get mixed up," Wilson warns.

"Right!"

Wilson and Charlie turn when they hear a siren. A black and white speeds up, and screeches to a halt, close to the yellow tape. It's John Spencer and a young Asian man.

Charlie walks to the tape to meet them. John ducks under the tape, and gives Charlie a friendly pat on the shoulder. "How's it going?"

"I just got here. The crime scene guy filled me in, but we're waiting for the M.E. It looks like the guy who owns the place got whacked over the head. Nasty wound. That's about all I know right now."

The Asian man shyly approaches and stops at a respectful distance. Charlie notices him and starts into her witness identification routing. "Male, Asian, about five-five, five-six. A hundred and ten pounds, black hair, blue business suit, brown shoes, maybe twenty-two—twenty-three years old."

She gives give John a questioning look, hunches her shoulders and turns her hands palms up.

"Oh yeah, this is your new partner, Charlie. This is Officer Mitchell Yen."

Mitchell manages a slight smile and steps forward. Charlie reaches over the tape to shake hands. His handshake is firmer than Charlie expected. "It's nice to meet you, Mitchell; we'll be seeing a lot of each other."

Mitchell Yen is of Chinese ancestry. He's only twenty-two years old, and has been on the police force a little more than a year. He was assigned as a traffic cop right out of the academy, and wasn't happy with the job. Traffic detail in Campbell, Ohio is not very rewarding. Mitchell Yen wants be a real cop. He's is well aware of Charlie Chandler and her accomplishments.

"I'm so happy to be working with you, Miss Chandler."

"Whoa," says Charlie, "stop right there. You call me Charlie, and I'll call you Mitchell. We won't have time for formalities. How does that sound?"

He smiles and nods.

Mitchell is small, but not all that small. Charlie is tall, but not all that tall. She's about five nine or ten. Somehow, she makes him look shorter than he is, and he makes her look taller than she is.

The business about the names almost brings Mitchell to tears. Fadler may not have heard of Charlie, but she has quite a reputation with the real cops. Mitchell is genuinely thrilled to be working with *the* Charlie Chandler. He can hardly believe it.

"Oh, Mitchell," says Charlie, "are you Chinese?"

"Why, yes I am."

Charlie fishes out her medallion and holds it up for Mitchell to read. "Can you tell me what this says?"

Mitchell steps up to look, being careful not to touch her.

"I can't read that stuff."

"But you're Chinese, aren't you?"

"Yeah, but I was adopted by an American couple, so I never even learned Chinese. It causes me all kinds of grief when I go out for a Chinese dinner. They actually get mad at me. The more I can't understand, the madder they get. I guess they think I'm fooling with them."

"What about your name, Yen. Isn't that Chinese?"

"Oh, my folks are Jewish and their name was difficult to pronounce here in the states, so they shortened it to Yen. It worked out."

Charlie put the charm back. "Let's get to work. Mitchell. I'd like you to keep notes for our report. You know the format?"

Mitchell pulls a small note pad from his coat pocket and proudly holds it up.

"Got it," he says.

Charlie looks Mitchell up and down. "You got a buzzer?"

Mitchell quickly feels his pockets. He finds his badge and holds it out proudly.

Charlie motions to hers, hanging from her breast pockets, and says, "Put it on."

Hurriedly, Mitchell put the badge in his breast pocket. He takes note of how Charlie has hers, and he's careful to adjusts his to be the same.

Charlie notices. She smiles. She likes him.

Charlie steps off toward the body. "Let's take a look-see."

Mitchell ducks under the tape and follows along in Charlie's footsteps. John Spencer tags along.

"Well there's the victim, Mitchell."

Mitchell's expression reveals that this is his first brush with violent death. He wonders if he's going to be sick.

Charlie notices and asks, "You gonna be okay?"

"I'll be okay," is his half-hearted answer.

Charlie turns to Wilson, who is packing up his stuff.

"What got him?"

"Somebody didn't like him—big time. It looks to me like they used a two by four to take off the back of his skull. It must have been one hell of a whack. I think it was a single blow—nice and clean. I'd look for somebody big—tall; somebody really powerful; a heavyweight. Of course, that's just my opinion; you hafta ask the M.E. for the official call."

Charlie nods and turns to Mitchell. "Hear that? Somebody big; somebody powerful to make that kind of wound."

Mitchell nods and writes on his pad.

"Could it have been a baseball bat?" asks Mitchell.

"I don't think so," replies Wilson, "the wound is too sharp, too neat and clean. Anyway, baseball bats don't leave splinters. We checked around the place and couldn't find a murder weapon...no baseball bat or board. You'll have to figure that one out. We did find wood fragments, so I know it was a piece of wood. In a couple of hours, I'll be able to tell you what kind of wood; maybe if it had paint on it."

The victim is William (Wild Bill) Fairall. He joined the carnival as a kid and stayed until he owned it. It wouldn't take an accountant to realize that the place couldn't make much money. Everything was worn, and dirty, and shabby. The only bright spot was that old circus wagon. The restaurant didn't look too bad; a new coat of white paint would do wonders. The wagon was well cared for and in perfect condition; the rest of the place was pretty sad.

Charlie sizes up the body. White. About six feet, 240 pounds. A good sized man; a nice looking fellow. Neat dresser. Expensive business suit; expensive shoes—highly polished. Pushing fifty, but it was hard to tell with the condition of the back of his head.

Charlie studies the ground near the body. Mitchell watches closely. "No blood," she says, and then she adds a bid of Charlie Chan wisdom. "Murder without bloodstains like Amos without Andy—most unusual."

"Who are Amos and Andy?" ask Mitchell.

Charlie realizes that Amos and Andy were in her father's time. Mitchell couldn't know.

"Hmmmmm. How about like Sonny and Cher?"

Mitchell is puzzled. "Who?"

"How old are you?" asks Charlie.

"Twenty-two, last Wednesday."

"Okay, murder without bloodstains like a hamburger without fries. It's an old Charlie Chan aphorism."

"Oh," smiles Mitchell, "I get it...aphorism?"

"It's a fancy name for a short saying. Charlie Chan used them in the old movies. I like them."

Mitchell nods like he has learned the secret of life.

Wilson gathers up his last piece of equipment and turns to Charlie. "By the way, he had cocaine in his blood—lots of it. No booze, just the white stuff. He was a big-time user."

Charlie nods. Mitchell Yen writes that down.

Charlie turns to Wilson. "Who's in charge around here? Does somebody run the place or is that him on the ground?"

Wilson points to a man standing at the entrance of the big tent. "That guy. His name is Barker. He's the sideshow barker. Barker the barker. Get it? He'll tell you about it. Again and again."

"Got it. When will I get your report?"

"Later today. I can e-mail it to you. Got a laptop?" says Wilson.

"I'll have Mitchell drop by later and pick it up." She makes a mental note: *Get a laptop.*

John Spencer starts toward his car.

"I gotta go. Fadler might stop by later. He asked about you."

Charlie and Mitchell watch as the cruiser pulls away. About half way to the main gate, the siren comes on.

Passing John's cruiser on the way out is the Medical Examiner's long black hearse on the way in. The driver is dressed in jeans and a short white lab coat. The passenger, dressed in a business suit, steps out and surveys the place. The driver carries a small black bag—the kind doctors used to carry back when they made house calls. Charlie can't help notice how much the gentleman in the suit looks like he belongs in a suit; some men don't. He's Doctor Murray Kidwell, the Medial Examiner.

Charlie puts her witness database in action. White, tall—about six one or two, a hundred and eight pounds, maybe thirty-five years old, dark brown hair, green eyes, glasses. A very nice looking guy; very nice.

The M.E. ducks under the tape and walks toward Wilson. "Hi, Jerry, what have you got here?"

Wilson walks over to stand nearby the body. Wilson, the Medial Examiner, and his technician go to work. All three get close to the body and exchange mumbled thoughts. The fellow in the white coat squats down to get a closer look. He gently moves Fairall's head from side to side, examining the wound, and gets up nodding his head, but without saying a word.

"Looks pretty simple to me. Off hand, I'd say he was on the wrong end of a two by four. It's too smooth for a pipe or baseball bat. I'll know better after I get him in the morgue," says Kidwell. "Did you find a weapon?"

Wilson shakes his head. "We checked the area pretty close, and didn't see anything. The body had definitely been moved."

Kidwell nods, and then looks at Charlie. He spots her badge and decides that she's the lead detective on the case. He takes a step forward and offers his hand. "I'm Murray Kidwell. I'll bet that you've already guessed that I'm the M.E."

Charlie shakes his hand and can't help saying, "Yeah, I guessed, but that sign on the side of your—uh—van gave you away."

Wilson, the M.E. and Charlie chuckle.

"You finished?" asks Kidwell.

"Yeah, I'm packing up now."

He turns to Charlie. "Can I have the body now?"

Charlie is surprised. "Are you asking me?"

"I can't take the body until you say it's okay."

"I'm sorry, this is my first murder case, and I wasn't aware of that."

"No problem; live and learn. The body can't leave until the lead detective gives the word."

While they have been talking, the man in the white coat wheels out a gurney and lowers it beside the body. Without speaking, Kidwell and the technician pick up Fairall and stretch it out on the gurney. He's covered with a sheet and strapped in place. The technician wheels the body to the edge of the crime scene tape. Kidwell approaches Charlie.

Mitchell watches the whole scene with wide eyes and slack jaw.

"Why don't you come down to the morgue this afternoon? We don't have a backlog now, so I should have something for you after lunch."

Charlie is unsure of what she should say. "Yeah, I guess that's good. That's okay. I'll be there."

The technician hands Charlie a clipboard and pen. The form on the board reads "Release Authorization."

Charlie scans the form. It's authorization to remove a body and take it to the morgue.

"If I don't sign, do I get to keep him?" she jokes.

The technician smirks. He's heard that one before. Charlie signs the form on the line marked "Lead Case Detective" and hands the clipboard back to the technician. Without saying a word, he tosses it on top of Fairall's body and starts wheeling it toward the hearse.

"Good luck on the new job," says Kidwell as he leaves.

"Thanks," answers Charlie. "I'll see you after lunch." Then she calls him back. "One more thing, does your assistant talk?"

"Don't get him started. He's a little shy around women, but normally he drives me nuts. See you after lunch."

The morgue; after lunch. Oh my God!

Charlie watches as the hearse pulls away. She looks at the guy standing by the tent, and heads off to meet Bart Barker.

Outside the Show Tent – Monday, 6/18, 1115 hrs.

Charlie walks toward the Show Tent and Barker. Mitchell follows close behind, making certain that he's in step with Charlie. Over her shoulder, Charlie gives Mitchell an instruction, "Check with John Spencer and find out how we can get a laptop. Wireless."

"Done."

Barker sees Charlie and Mitchell coming. He takes a deep breath and tells himself, "Here we go."

Bart Barker extends his hand as Charlie approaches. She pauses before deciding to accept his hand shake.

"Bart Baker, miss. I'm the barker for the show. Bart Barker the barker. Isn't that great?"

Charlie knows that he must pull this routine on everyone he meets.

"Hmmmm. Yeah...great. Are you in charge?"

"Yes, ma'am. More than that; I was the junior partner in the business with Fairall, but it's all mine now."

That remark startles Charlie.

"Aren't you a little fast on the draw? The guy's only been dead a few hours."

"Well, we each had a will that leaves everything to the survivor. I guess I own the whole works now."

Charlie disliked Barker the second she shook hands with him.

"If I were you, I'd check with a good lawyer and the court before I spent any money."

"It better be mine!" says an angry Barker.

"I'd like to ask you a few questions," says Charlie.

"Am I a suspect?"

"Everybody's a suspect until I find the bad guy."

Just then, an old man pushing a strange looking cart passes by.

"Morning, Fred," says Barker.

"Mornin'," replies Fred.

Barker motions for Fred to stop and come over.

"This is a detective, Fred; she's looking into Fairall's death."

He tries to introduce her, but has forgotten her name already. "This is Miss uh, uh. Did you tell me your name?"

"Chandler. Detective Chandler."

"Yeah, well this is Fred Doer, our maintenance guy. Fred has been with us for years and years."

"Mornin', ma'am," says Fred with a tip of his hat and slight bow.

Charlie nods and steps closer to the cart. Mitchell joins in and they walk around it, wondering about all the things hanging on the sides. Every available square inch is covered with a tool or material. On the front are mail-box type letters, "USS Kearsarge."

"This is my maintenance cart," says Fred proudly. "My baby. I designed it myself," he continues, "built it too." Fred continues with his presentation. "Those are wheels off a Kawasaki bike—balloon tires—she rides nice and smooth. I've got stuff on here to take care of all the rides and just about anything else. I'll bet NASA could use an idea like this. You folks work with NASA?"

Before Charlie can answer, Fred continues his monologue. "Would you believe there's a compressor inside? And on the front, here, is a little generator in case I need these lights." He points to a couple of pipes pointing up with flood lights attached.

"Wasn't the Kearsarge a Navy ship—an aircraft carrier or something?" asks Charlie.

Fred's eyes light up. Yes, ma'am! My ol' ship. She goes way back in the eighteen hundreds. I wasn't on *that* one." He shakes his head and smiles, lost in fond memories.

"Does it play music?" jokes Mitchell.

"No, but that's not a bad idea..." Fred searches around for a space. "Maybe I could mount speakers on a bracket." He scratches his chin. "Hummm..."

"Well," smiles Charlie, "Mister Doer, it's a wonderful machine, I'm impressed." Charlie feels obligated to ask questions about the cart. "What are these two pipes sticking out the front?"

"Well, they are just pipes now, but I sent away for some halogen lights that will fit in those." He pauses to think. "You know what halogens are?"

"No, I don't," answers Charlie.

"I don't either, but they looked real sharp in the catalog," says Fred.

Fred Doer smiles and shows his pleasure with all the attention. He gives his cart an affectionate pat and starts on his way.

"Don't you want to question him?" asks Barker.

Charlie studies Fred Doer as he walks away. *He's at least 75, tall, thin, gray hair, of course, stands straight, not stooped like some. In pretty good shape for an old guy. He wears one of those all-purpose dark blue uniforms with his name on a patch on the pocket. He's soft-spoken, and seems like a very nice person—a little too wrapped up in his work, and maybe off a little in the head.*

"I'll get him later," she lies. Questioning that nice old guy would be like questioning her grandpa.

Charlie motions for Mitchell to come close. She makes a little sign like writing on her hand. Mitchell picks up on it right away and pulls out his pad.

Charlie takes the 3 X 5 cards out of her pocket. Holding them like a winning poker hand, she asks her questions:

"Did Fairall have any enemies?"

"Not that I know of, but *somebody* must have had it in for him."

"Was he into drugs?"

"Wild Bill? Naw, he was straight as an arrow."

Mitchell and Charlie exchange knowing glances.

"Did he have any unusual habits or vices?"

"He spent every second of his life trying to keep this show from folding. I don't know if that's a hobby or a vice. He was a workaholic."

"Did he like boys, or girls?"

"If he was here, he'd be hitting on you. That's why they called him Wild Bill."

"Did he hang out with any bad people?"

"You mean besides me?"

Charlie's face sours. "Yeah, besides you."

"I never saw him with anybody."

"Married?"

"Four times, I think. His alimony could make the payroll."

"Okay, how much money did Fairall owe you?"

"How'd you know he owed me money?"

"I'm a detective—remember? How much?"

"I've lost track."

"Okay, anyone fired recently?"

"Fired? Our turnover is zero. This ain't McDonalds. Where you gonna hire someone who weighs eight hundred pounds, or someone who is two and a half feet tall?"

Barker points to the giant poster lining the walls of the big show tent. Look at all those star attractions. The World's Tallest Man; The World's Smallest Human; The African Rubber Man; Henry the Hippo Boy; and..."

Charlie interrupts, "Okay, I get the idea. You've got a lot of...er...performers. When was the last time you saw Fairall?"

"A couple of hours ago. I found the body."

"I mean alive."

Scratching the back of his neck, Barker says, "Well, I'm not sure what time it was. Yesterday...maybe after lunch. I'm sure about that."

Barker looks down at the ground and slowly shakes his head. Sadly he says, "All those attractions are gone now. These people get old and die just like everybody else. Anymore, we're just a retirement home with a Ferris wheel."

"Let's get back to the money question. How much money did Fairall owe you?"

"A bunch! I don't really know the exact amount. If a guy shorts your pay for a couple years, and it adds up, you lose track. He kept telling me that I could take it out of the profit when he was gone."

"Gone?"

"Dead! He was always talking about dying...getting knocked off. I never paid much attention to that; I just figured it was his way of delaying things so he wouldn't have to settle up."

"Delay is the deadliest form of denial," says Charlie.

"Wow," exclaims Mitchell. "Was that Charlie Chan?"

"No, Parkinson's law."

"Who's Parkinson?"

"Like Yogi says, you could look it up."

"Who's Yogi?"

"Never mind."

Mitchell gives a confused nod, and turns back to his notes.

Charlie returns to Barker. "I get it. Where do you hang out? I'll want to talk with you later."

Barker points to the circus wagon. "I'll either be over there in the office, or in the main show tent. I have an apartment in there. Right down the middle, all the way in the back. Mine is a small world. Look behind the Elephant Man." He walks away, toward the circus wagon.

Charlie thinks, *Elephant Man?*

She puts Barker in her member bank. *White male, six one or two, two twenty—two thirty pounds, reddish hair, tight wave, freckles, wild clothes—loud plaid coat and matching trousers, running shoes, show off.*

"That's gotta be a costume," she says out loud to herself.

"One more thing," Charlie yells to Barker. "I want this whole circus shut down and locked up. This is a crime scene."

Barker moans, "You can't do that. We'll have people pouring in here in a little while. We have a show to do."

"No show today, Mister Barker, it's lock-down time...and I mean it."

Charlie motions to Mitchell to give her his notes. He hands them over and she checks them as they walk along. Out of range of Barker, Mitchell says, "That guy thinks he's a big shot."

"Mouse cannot cast the shadow of an elephant," says Charlie.

Mitchell is impressed. "Wow, is that a Chan aphorism?"

"From *The Black Camel.* Excellent. Good job." She hands the pad back to Mitchell. "Run up there to the gate and string tape all over the place. Use plenty of tape, and see if they have any traffic cones you can put out. See that yellow Volks up there?"

Mitchell nods.

"On the way back, check my glove compartment and get my little camera."

She tosses him her keys, and he starts off but then stops. He turns to Charlie. "We don't have any crime scene tape."

"Oh...great! Go over there and see if Mister Wilson will loan us a few rolls."

Mitchell takes off on a run.

Baker stops on his journey to the wagon. He turns back to Charlie and motions to the restraint. "Want a cup of coffee? Carrie makes the best."

Charlie thinks for a second and nods. She knows this guy is a con and wants to con her into something. "Yeah, that would go good. Wait till my partner gets back."

They each think that they have somehow outsmarted the other.

Moments later, Mitchell arrives, camera in hand, panting hard. They head for the restaurant.

Carrie's Restaurant – Monday, 6/21 – 1255 hrs.

Charlie looks at her watch, and looks at the restaurant. She realizes that this building is probably in better shape than anything else in the park. Barker pulls the old screen door open, and holds it while Charlie and Mitchell walk in. The screen door slams behind Barker. Charlie has a sudden memory of her grandmother's kitchen. Grandma's door sounded just like that. She felt a tinge of sadness.

Charlie checks the place out. Clean; neat; right out of the forties or early fifties. A long counter with white porcelain stools, seat-backs with shiny brass spindles. A back-bar full of round mirrors and paper signs announcing the price of various items. At the check-out counter is a huge old brass NCR cash register with a giant crank handle protruding from one side. The wall behind the cash register is covered with framed black-and-white photos.

A few people are eating.

All the tables and chairs are old; no two alike.

Barker, Charlie, and Mitchell take a seat at one of the old tables.

"This place is something else!" says Charlie.

Barker smiles. "Yeah, it's run by Carrie Sheppard, wife of the original park owner. When he died, Fairall took over the park, and let Carrie have the restaurant free and clear. Knowing Fairall, he somehow got the best of the deal. She does an incredible job…and with only the help of a few college kids. She cooks, cleans, waits table, and runs the cash register. Oh yeah, and takes out the garbage. Quite a woman. Most of the people who come to the park come to eat here, not for the rides or the show."

Just then, the louvered double doors to the kitchen swing open, and Carrie Sheppard walks out holding a tray with cups, saucers, and a pot of coffee.

Charlie switches on her witness computer. *Carrie is about sixty, maybe sixty-five years old. Her gray-streaked hair is tied back in a bun. Wire-rim glasses, no makeup, no jewelry. She's small, maybe five two, and slightly plump. Not fat; plump. She wears a dark blue dress with tiny flower prints. Her running shoes don't seem to fit the image, but Charlie realizes that Carrie must do a lot of on-the-job walking. She's the Norman Rockwell picture of everybody's grandmother.*

"You folks look like you could use some coffee." Carrie flashes her irresistible smile, and everybody smiles back. Carrie sets out the cups and starts to pour. She turns to Charlie. "Are you the police lady I've been hearing about?"

"Well, I am a police lady." Charlie nods. She wonders how the word could have gotten out so fast. She's hardly talked to anyone. "Would you have time to answer some questions for me?"

Carrie is thrilled. This is the first break in her routine since she can't remember when.

"Oh, yes. I'd be happy to."

"First," Charlie says, "I'd like to know how you knew we would like coffee."

"I've been running this restaurant for almost forty years now. I've picked up a few ideas about what people want."

Charlie turns to Barker. "I wonder if you would excuse us for a few minutes. Police business—you know how it is."

Barker realizes that he doesn't have a choice. He smiles, jumps up, grabs his coffee and heads for the door.

"I'll bring the cup back later, Carrie. I'll be in the wagon if you need me," and with that he's gone. The old screen door slams again.

Charlie sips her coffee. Carrie anxiously waits. Mitchell has his note pad at the ready.

"I think this is the best coffee I've ever had. I'm no Starbucks fan. Theirs tastes bitter to me. This is good; excellent."

Carrie busts with pride but doesn't speak. She pulls out a chair and sits down next to Charlie.

"What can you tell me about Mister Fairall, Miss Sheppard?"

"Call me Carrie, dear. Everyone calls me Carrie."

"Okay, Carrie. What can you tell me about Mister Fairall?"

"Well, he tried his best to keep the place running. I've known him since he was just a kid. He wasn't always the nicest man. Sometimes he would go into a real rant about some little thing. I guess he had a lot on his mind."

Carrie slides her chair closer to Charlie. He voice drops into a whisper.

"Sometimes I think he was on something." She winks. "Know what I mean?"

Charlie nods. "Did he hang out with any bad people that you know about?"

"Well, I'm not sure if they were bad people, but sometimes he'd have some strange looking people in for dinner. One man really looked suspicious to me. He'd never look you in the eye, and they would always talk real low. If I were to walk to their table, the conversation would stop. Sometimes I saw them hand envelopes and small packages back and forth. Just like on TV. I like *CSI Miami.*"

"I do too," says Charlie. "Do you know what was in the envelopes and packages?"

"Oh, no, I didn't know and I wouldn't ask. It was their business."

"Was it always the same person who met with him, or were there lots of men?"

"Different men, but mainly this one gentleman. One time there was a woman, but it was just that one time. She looked like a show girl to me. Kind of trashy, you know what I mean? Too much makeup, too few clothes. You know the type…her clothes say 'look at me,' and when the men do, she says, 'what you are looking at?'"

"What did this man look like, the one who was a regular?"

"Well, he wasn't very tall, and he was a little overweight, I'd say. He was dark, and always needed a shave. I think he might have been Italian, or maybe Greek. I'm not good at recognizing people's races." Carrie leans back in her chair and points to the wall behind the cash register. "There's a picture of him on that wall."

Charlie jumps up. "Picture? Let's take a look."

She waits while Carrie gets up. Carrie knows she keeps people waiting sometimes. "I'm not quite as fast as I used to be." She stands and both knees let out an audible *click*. "Come on, I'll show you the picture. Then I have to beg off to take care of those people. It'll just take a minute."

Charlie and Mitchell follow Carrie. The picture was one of those snap shots of people sitting at a booth, dirty plates and glasses in front of them, all are mugging for the camera. Carrie narrates the photo.

"That's my husband Fred, next to him is Bill Thompson. Bill got a job in California and this was his going away dinner. There's Mister Barker, next to him is the guy. I don't know his name. Does that help?"

"I don't really know, Carrie; we'll check this guy out." She turns to Mitchell. "You got my camera?"

Mitchell pulls a tiny digital camera from his breast pocket and answers with an enthusiastic, "Yep!"

"Get a shot of that picture. Get in as close as you can; I think that thing has a setting for close-ups. There…press that button with the flower."

"Got it," says Mitchell. He moves around getting set, and presses the button. There is a flash, and Mitchell looks at the camera screen. He's having trouble.

"Set it to 'play,'" says Charlie.

Mitchell fumbles around and finally, accidentally sets the tiny device to play, but is surprised when he sees the picture. With a sickening look, he holds the camera out for Charlie to see. Nothing but a white screen.

Charlie is careful not to hurt Mitchell's feelings.

"Try it again. This time without the flash, and stand at a slight angle so you don't get the reflection of yourself in the glass."

Mitchell follows her instructions, and the picture is great. He holds the camera up for Charlie to see. "Aren't these things amazing?"

"Amazing," says Charlie.

Mitchell and Charlie head back to the table. Carrie is taking care of her customers. The two detectives examine the photos. Carrie joins them. Charlie picks up where she left off.

"How much money did Fairall owe you?"

"Say, you are a good detective. How'd you know that?"

Charlie smiles. "What kind of detective would I be if I didn't? Could you tell me about that?"

Carrie is puzzled at that remark. "Well, when Fred died, Mister Fairall offered to buy the place. He wanted the whole carnival; lock, stock, and barrel as they say. The property…the whole works. Fred was my husband. We set up the park when our show got stranded here.

"Anyway, Bill came to see me and asked if he could buy the place. I didn't see how I could run it so I told him to make an offer. He offered $750,000 and said I could have the restaurant. I didn't know what the business was worth, but I thought I could get by for a long time with the $750,000 and my social security. With that and running the restaurant, I figured I could make it. I live upstairs, so it works out well. The only problem I have is this darn knee. It takes me ten minutes to get up to my place anymore."

"Did he pay you the $750,000?"

"No. He was able to give me fifty thousand dollars up front, and the deal was that I would get the restaurant, and he would pay me twenty percent of the gross until it was paid off. We didn't figure in any interest or anything like that. I didn't want to get lawyers involved, and I didn't have any reason not to trust him. It was enough money for me."

"How much money did he owe you?"

"Seven hundred thousand bucks. I guess I won't be getting that now."

"Hmmm. Well, that's all for now, Carrie. I may have some more questions later. Maybe you should check with Barker about the money. If he inherited the business, he also inherited the debt."

"I'll do that. Won't you have some pie? I just pulled them out of the oven."

Mitchell's eyes light up. He's hungry.

"We'll have to pass right now, Carrie. Maybe we can come back another time."

"Oh!" says Carrie, "you didn't tell me your name."

"I'm sorry, how rude of me. My name is Charlie. Charlie Chandler. This is my partner, Officer Mitchell Yen." Mitchell smiles and nods.

Carrie thinks for a few seconds. "Charlie Chandler, a detective. Why it's almost like Charlie Chan in the old movies. You're probably too young to know about him."

Charlie can't help but chuckle. "Oh, I know about Charlie Chan okay. My dad was a detective and sometimes they called him Charlie Chan. We used to watch the old movies."

"Isn't that interesting? Your dad was a detective, and now you're one. I bet he's proud."

"Yeah, I guess it's a family business. I hope I can be half as good at it as he was. You're a cool lady, Carrie—very up-to-date."

"Well," says Carrie, "I'm from a different era, but not a different planet."

Charlie laughs, and she and Mitchell say their goodbyes. Charlie offers money for the coffee, but Carrie waves her off.

"By the way, Carrie, I'd like it if you called me Charlie."

"I'd like that," answers Carrie.

They leave the restaurant.

Charlie motions to Mitchell. "It's time for us to visit Mister Fairall at the morgue. You ready?"

Mitchell gives a hesitant nod.

"Let's go. We can also drop that picture off with the narcotics people and see if they know the guy. I'll bet he's a dealer."

Charlie decides that she better do something about her suit and the heat. "I'm going to run over to the mall tonight and pick up a few things. We'll start again in the morning."

The yellow Volkswagen drives past the sleeping guard.

Charlie's House – Monday, 6/21 – 1830 hrs.

Charlie and Mom have finished dinner and are watching TV in the living room. They have matching Lazy Boy chairs sitting side by side with the foot rests up. Both of them have a remote. The TV, a very large flat screen model, is about eight feet away. It's really too big for the room. It took Mom a long time to get used to the large screen, but she learned to like it.

43

"Don't you get tired of the news, Mom?"

"I want to know what's going on, but I try not to let it get me down."

"The way I figure it, everybody knows the same thing."

Mom's cat, named Groucho because he has a black mustache, crawls up on Charlie's lap.

"We already had dinner, Groucho. Didn't you eat?"

Groucho purrs and rubs his head on Charlie's arm.

Mom looks over from her chair." Tell me about your day, Charlie. It's kind of odd to start off a new job with a murder case, isn't it?"

"Fadler said that I was the only one he could spare. Can you imagine? Spare! I'm the only one in the entire police department that's so unimportant that he can spare me. Maybe he was right. I felt like an idiot talking to the medical examiner. I'll never forget how Doctor Kidwell helped me. He's a pretty sharp guy."

"Oh, I don't think Fadler meant it that way, Charlie. I think it just means that everyone was tied up on something, and you weren't. You're making too much of it."

"I guess I'm just worried. This amusement park is nutty, full of characters. Do you know they have a guy who weighs eight hundred pounds?"

Mom shakes her head and smiles.

"Noooo. I don't think so."

"Did Dad have any rough cases?"

"None worse that what you're telling me about. He just kept plugging away till he had his bad guy in handcuffs. I'll tell you the truth, sometimes he didn't know how he solved a case. He said it was blind luck. If he had a problem, he'd sleep on it. In the morning, he'd have an answer. That's the way he operated."

Charlie liked to hear that. She wonders what it would be like to have Dad around to help her. "I'm not sure I'm doing the right thing. I'm floundering around. I don't want to fail, Mom. I don't want to let Dad down."

"You're your own person, Charlie. You have to do things for yourself and not for your dad. That's the way it works. You're not going to fail."

"I've go to do something about my suit. I don't think I can wear jeans and t-shirt, but my new suit is too hot."

Mom thinks for a couple of seconds. "Why don't you get some wash pants—slacks, and wear a long shirt?"

"The slacks would probably be okay, but a long shirt would make it hard to get to my gun...or to let somebody know that I have a gun."

"Just get a plain blouse, short-sleeves, and a light jacket. Get stuff you can wash out."

Charlie jumps up and tosses Groucho back on the chair. "I'm going to run over to the mall and get an outfit right now. You want to come along?"

"Right now?"

"Right now. I'm gonna hit the mall and get back here to hit the sack. I've got a busy day tomorrow. Maybe I'll have the answer when I wake up, like Dad. I told Mitchell I'd pick him up at Oh Eight Hundred, in front of the headquarters building. We'll drive to the morgue from there."

"You people and that military time...oh eight hundred, honestly."

Charlie gives Mom a kiss, drops Groucho in her lap and starts for the mall."

Jackson County Morgue – Tuesday, 6/22 – 0820 hrs.

Charlie pulls into the "Visitor" parking spot in the front of the big gray stone building. At one time, the building housed the County government, the sheriff, and the jail. The cornerstone was laid in 1830. Now, except for the morgue in the basement, it's vacant.

Mitchell can't help but notice Charlie's new outfit: Khaki slacks, white shirt, and light jacket to cover her gun. She wears her badge on a long chain over her neck. *Cool*, thinks Mitchell. He wonders how he would look in the same outfit.

Mitchell pulls the big brass handles on the big brass door. They exchange glances of surprise when it opens so easily. They walk in. After only a few steps, they find themselves standing in a very large, very dark lobby. Polished stone floors, walls covered with unlit display

45

cases full of awards and trophies, and a couple of life-size statues.

Suddenly, the place lights up. Florescent lights flicker as they start up all over the room. Directly in front of them, an ornate brass elevator door slides open and Doctor Murray Kidwell steps out.

"Quite the place, huh?"

Charlie is mesmerized. "I've never seen anything like it."

"It's a showplace, but we're then only ones here now. It's a good-news, bad-news thing. We're kind of forgotten by the rest of the government, but wait until you see my office. The people who built this thing went first class when it came to their offices. I guess things were cheaper back in the 1830s. He turns and waves for them to follow.

Doctor Kidwell leads Charlie and Mitchell down a long marble hall lined with even more trophy cases. Charlie tries to stop her heels from clicking on the marbled surface by walking on her toes. They pause in front a large double-door at the very end of the hall. Kidwell holds his index finger to his lip. "Shhhhh."

He pushes one door open and flicks the light switch. This is not an office; this is a cathedral. The room had to be at least twenty feet wide and a good thirty feet long. The ceiling was at least twelve feet high. A gigantic oriental carpet covered a fifteen-foot-wide path to the heavily carved desk. Charlie is awestruck. That carpet must be worth a hundred thousand dollars, even if it's a fake. There's nothing to say.

Kidwell smiles. "I see you're impressed."

He walks around the desk and stands beside the high-back chair. "Actually, I don't do much work up here. It's very lonely, and I think the place is haunted. If you try to work here, you'll hear all kinds of strange noises. I think I've seen a real ghost."

"It's spectacular," says Charlie.

Mitch nods his agreement.

Kidwell walks to a corner of the room and reaches behind a stack of books on the bookshelf. There is a hum, and one bookcase swings out. Kidwell smiles as he watches his guests' expressions.

"Secret passage," he says, and waves for them to come along.

It's a tiny elevator! They all crowd in and Kidwell pulls the bookcase-door closed. He slides the brass elevator door shut, and moves a large control lever to one side. The thing starts moving. After what seems an eternity, it stops. Kidwell opens the elevator door and turns the knob on what looks like a pretty normal door. It opens into a large dimly lit room full of stainless steel sinks, table, and cabinets. It is the county morgue.

Kidwell steps forward, turns and stops, waiting for the others to follow.

"That's an old secret passage from the Civil War. It used to have a spiral staircase, but that was replaced with a hydraulic elevator about nineteen thirty something. The elevator is just like the lift at the garage that lifts your car. It's pretty neat, but I only use it to show off for guests. It's too slow." He flicks a wall switch, and the room lights up.

The first thing that catches Charlie's eye is the body of William Fairall stretched out on a stainless steel table. He's naked except for a folded sheet covering his private parts. Her first thought is that the table looks so cold. She has to remind herself that Fairall is dead; he can't feel the cold.

Not exactly certain of her role in this whole process, she quietly follows Doctor Kidwell to the table.

"Well, there he is. It's pretty simple, blunt force trauma to the head. He has some cocaine in his system, but that didn't kill him. It had to be something with a relatively shape edge. I think Wilson may be right...it was probably a two by four."

Charlie takes a deep breath and tightens her stomach; she steps forward to look at the body.

"What are those bruises on his chest?"

"I'm not sure what caused those, but they didn't contribute to his death."

"It may sound silly to you, Doctor, but what do I do now?" Charlie asks.

The Doctor gives a sympathetic nod. "There isn't anything more for you do to here; that is, unless you have some questions." Charlie shakes her head and gives Mitchell a questioning look. He shrugs and shakes his head.

"No, I don't have anything now. Do you send me the autopsy report?"

"You'll get the autopsy and photos. If you have any questions, I'd be happy to help you."

"Well, okay, I guess that does it. I want to thank you for your help...and the tour."

"Glad to help. I'll show you out...the normal way out."

They push through the stainless steel covered doors and start up the stairs. Charlie takes in the sight. Even the stairs are like a palace or something. There are about ten steps to a platform, and then it splits into two sets of stairs leading to the main floor. Doctor Kidwell accompanies Charlie and Mitchell to the front door. They shake hands all around, and head back to the car.

"Well, let's head back to the funny farm and talk with the performers. Maybe we can figure this thing out."

Around The Park – Tuesday, 6/22 – 1123 hrs.

Charlie parks the yellow Volks close to the circus wagon, in a no parking zone. She knows that she's the only cop around, but slips the "Official Police Business" sign in the window anyway.

Mitchell is thinking about the restaurant. He didn't eat breakfast and his stomach is growling. "You afraid of getting a ticket?" He chuckles.

"No, but it might keep bad people from messing with my car. Come on, partner; let's take a walk around this joint so we can figure out how it works."

The two start their unguided inspection tour. A few people have tried to come in the park, but the yellow tape stopped them. Mitchell looks back at the restaurant longingly.

Two people, with their little kids, sneaked in the back way, through Carrie's restaurant. They had breakfast and then came out to the rides. The place doesn't normally open until noon, so they slipped the kid who runs the rides five bucks and he let the kids on. Charlie decides not to bother them.

They stop and look at a kiddy ride. Small brightly painted cars go round and round on a flat track. Like everything else, they look like they have been painted hundreds of times.

"Not very exciting," Charlie comments.

There are only two kids on the ride. Proud parents wave at their kid as they pass by. One rider, a little boy, just sits staring ahead with his nose running. The little girl rider turns the steering wheel like she's in the Grand Prix. Charlie can't help but wonder how long these cars could last. They must be pre-World War Two.

Mitchell notices that the ride operator left one ride running and moved to another one. He taps Charlie's arm to get her attention.

"Check the wheels on that silver car."

Charlie looks. It takes a second, but she realizes that the little car only has three wheels. She shakes her head.

They walk on to a ride where airplane looking things hang on chains, and swing around. They look more like boxes with wings than airplanes. Some have tin propellers that look like they were taken from old fans. Only one child is riding, and his parents stand looking at him like he just graduated from college. The kid waves each time he passes his folks. Suddenly, he's sick and throws up all over his boxy airplane…inside and out.

Mitchell turns away. Apologetically he tells Charlie, "If they go I go."

The college kid operating the ride shakes his head and curses. He yanks the switch to turn the thing off, and heads for the hose. He doesn't check the car ride to see if it's still running, or if a kid's in trouble.

"Should I tell him to shut down and send the kids home?"

"No, they'll be gone soon; don't make a stink. You say something and the parents will fly into a rage and eat up our time."

They continued their tour.

"What are we looking for?" asks Mitchell.

"I don't know exactly. Clues I guess. I just want to get a feel for the place. The size, how stuff is taken care of, that short of thing. I wonder how many people work here, and which one of them would whack Fairall."

Mitchell scans the scene. "So far, it doesn't look like anything is well taken care of. Look at the kiddy rides. Missing wheels; one college kid to run two rides. Not good. I'd think the State would crack down on this kind of stuff."

Charlie nods. "Let's take a look at that Ferris wheel."

The Ferris wheel turns slowly. There are no riders, but it's left running to attract attention...let people know that the park is open, even though it isn't.

They walk around the wheel, looking up most of the time.

A voice screams out, "Hey, watch your step!"

Startled, Charlie jumps back. They look around.

"Down here. I'm trying to take a sun bath."

Charlie looks down and sees a tiny man in a bathing suit stretched out on a towel. He can't be more than two and a half, maybe three feet tall, very muscular, but not well formed.

Mitchell is surprised. "Look, a midget."

The little man screams, "Little person, little person, you ugly gook!"

Mitchell is not offended because he's never heard the term "gook."

Charlie keeps her cool. "Do you work here?"

"Work here? Hell, I'm the one who keeps this place going. I've been running this wheel for fifteen years. Without me, this place is history."

"Where do you live?"

"Who are you, anyway?"

Charlie holds out her badge. "Police. We're here about the Fairall thing."

"Yeah, how about that. I live over there. They got me jammed in that crappy sideshow tent—next to Barker. He sits in there drinking that cheap Scotch and plays that damn record player all night. All night! I gotta move."

"Are you part of the show?" Charlie asks.

"Am I part of the show...how many times to I have to tell you, lady? I AM the show!" He gives Mitchell a nasty look. "I'm not a midget. Actually, I'm a dwarf. There's a big difference. We're a cut above the midgets, and I don't have anything to do with those freaks. They'd love to put me up on that stage with those weirdos. Barker wants me to be Jojo, dog-faced boy. Can you imagine?"

Charlie points to her badge. "We're here investigating Mr. Fadler's murder. I have a few questions I'd like to ask you, and I'm taking DNA samples."

"Ask away, but you're not going to take my DNA," barks the dwarf. "You got a warrant?"

"Do I need one? We're doing this to eliminate suspects. Is there some reason that we shouldn't look at your DNA?"

The dwarf wraps his towel around his shoulders. He's obviously not pleased with this.

"What do I have to do?"

Charlie opens a tube and takes out the swab. "Just say Ahhhh."

The dwarf swears a little under his breath, then says, "Ahhhhhhh..." and as Charlie removes the swab he adds, "Shit!" He laughs a real belly-laugh. "Aww shit, get it?"

"You nasty little man."

Charlie puts the swab in the tube, caps it and writes "Midget" on the label. She holds it down so the dwarf can see the word midget."

"Little people. Little people, you overgrown Barbie doll. I gotta get dressed. I'll have riders in a few minutes."

"Not today, little man," says Mitchell. "The park is closed until we finish up."

"Closed? Nobody told *me*!"

"I'm telling you now. We'll check back with you about those questions," says Charlie.

The dwarf just waves them off and starts putting on his clothes.

They continue around the wheel.

"Boy, is that little guy something, or is that little guy something?" says Mitchell.

"One small wind can raise much dust." Charlie smiles.

"Charlie Chan?"

She nods and smiles. "*Charlie Chan and the Dark Alibi.*"

They continue on.

Mitchell points to the old motor running the wheel. It was taken from a very old John Deere tractor. It still has the John Deere logo on the side. It's noisy and smelly.

"Boy, look at the old motor that runs this thing. I'll bet that baby is World War One surplus. Probably should be in the Smithsonian."

Charlie chuckles. "Check the ground around here," she tells Mitchell. "I hear people lose all sorts of things from their pockets. Maybe you can find your fortune."

"Hey," says Mitchell, "what's that?" He bends down and picks something up. "You mean like these?" He holds up a set of keys, about fifteen in all on a ring. Charlie takes the ring and examines it. "If these are car keys, some customer must still be sitting out in the parking lot." She examines each key.

Charlie instinctively looks around to see if someone has lost the keys. She looks back at the ground. She's startled. "Is that blood?"

Mitchell hurries over to look.

"Where?"

"There, on the grass. I think that's dried blood!"

Mitchell bends to take a better look.

"I don't know. I've never seen dried blood before. It's not very red."

"I'm sure it's blood. And if it's the right blood, our murder could have happened right where you're standing."

Mitchell looks down and takes a step backward. He doesn't like the idea of standing on the spot where a murder took place.

She puts one hand on Mitchell's shoulder and at a near whisper gives him instructions.

"Run over to the restaurant and ask Carrie for a couple of small plastic freezer bags; the kind with a zip top. Get back here fast; we need to B and T this stuff."

Mitchell takes off in a dead run.

Carrie is very helpful and gives Mitchell several bags, right out of the box. She can't help asking, "What are they for?"

Mitchell is already on his way out. With a slight squint and a hushed voice, he says, "We have to B and T some stuff."

Carrie just shakes her head and with a slight wave returns to the kitchen.

Mitchell arrives back at the Ferris wheel, bags in hand. He holds them out to Charlie. She takes one bag and bends down. With the tiny scissors in her little Swiss Army knife, she clips a few blades of the stained grass, and without touching them, scoops them into the bag. Mitchell watches in astonishment.

"Get your notebook. Write the date and 'found under Ferris wheel' on a sheet." He does and she says, "Slip the paper in the bag."

Charlie closes the bag.

"We've got to get this to the Crime Lab fast."

"I can run it over, but Charlie, what's B and T?"

"Bag and Tag, Mitchell."

"Oh," says Mitchell. "Cool." He nods. "B and T."

"Okay, take this bag to the Crime Lab. And take your picture to the Narc guys. See if they know the mystery man. Don't forget to bring my camera back. They can download the picture, but don't let them keep the camera."

"I don't have a ride. Mister Spencer drove me over, and he split. What should I do?"

Charlie fishes her car keys out of her pocket. Reluctantly she hands them to Mitchell. Like a mother talking to a teenage driver she says, "Here, take my car. Run this stuff to the crime lab. Find out if it's Fairall's blood."

"What if it's somebody else's blood?"

"I don't care about anybody else. If it's Fairall's blood, the murder took place here, and we're on to something. If it's not his, for all we know maybe somebody had a nose bleed. Take the car, and remember that it belongs to me, not the department. If it comes back with a single scratch, you're toast."

Mitchell's face shows his concern as he accepts the keys. He starts to leave when Charlie shouts, "Hey, you got a piece?"

"Piece? Piece of what?"

"Piece—Gun."

"No, we didn't carry a weapon in traffic."

"Stop by and see John Spencer. Tell him you need a gun, holster, and handcuffs. And tell him we need some DNA kits and a laptop computer. We need that laptop."

"What are we going to do with it?"

"I don't know, but we need it."

Mitchell waves a little salute and heads for the yellow Volkswagen going over an imaginary list in his mind. Charlie can't bear to watch someone else drive her little car.

Fun House – Tuesday, 6/22 – 1335 hrs.

Charlie decides to keep on looking for clues. She walks to the Fun House.

The Fun House is much like the big tent. There's a wooden skeleton covered with brightly painted canvas tent. It wouldn't hurt to trim the weeds growing around the edges. Who ever cuts the grass doesn't get very close to the tent. Near the entrance is a very old car. Charlie has never seen one like this, so she doesn't know what year it is. It's a convertible with a top in rags, long passed its prime. It's painted a cream color and all four tires are flat. It doesn't look inviting. She approaches the ticket booth, and put one hand on the little tray, under the barred window.

"How many?" says a voice.

Charlie is startled and jumps back from the booth. She just stands there, wondering. The door of the booth swings open and who steps out but Barker, the barker.

"Hey, little lady, want to try out the fun house?"

Charlie didn't like the little lady remark at all. The guy was definitely hitting on her, and her expression showed that she didn't like it. She felt like she had to say something.

"You sell tickets too?"

"I'm a man of many talents, my dear."

"You say 'little lady,' or 'my dear' one more time and I'll flatten you. Got it?"

Barker is shocked. All he can do is look at his shoes and nod. Charlie thinks he looks like a little kid. Trying to change the subject, he points to the car. "Have you seen my pride and joy?"

Charlie just looks. She's not interested, and doesn't have anything to say.

"It's a forty-one Plymouth convertible. Andy Hardy had one just like it in the old movies."

Charlie thinks, *Andy Hardy? Who the hell is Andy Hardy? Should I know that?*

"Does anybody work here? Who runs this spook house?"

"Not spook house. It's the Fun House now. We had to shut down the Spook House a couple of years back."

"So who runs it?"

"Well," says Barker, "nobody runs it. There isn't anything behind that canvas but junk. It used to have little cars that ran around, but we had to sell them off."

She would like for Barker to disappear. To avoid him, she turns and surveys the park. In the distance she sees her little Volkswagen pull past the guard shack. Mitchell parks the car in the very back of the empty lot, and starts walking toward Charlie.

Without another word, Charlie leaves Barker standing there, and starts walking toward her partner. As she walks by the Ferris wheel she notices the dwarf talking to a huge black man. They don't seem to notice her. The way they are acting, she's sure that they are up to no good. She's not sure, but she thinks she saw the big black man hand a small package to the dwarf. She thinks it looks like drug stuff.

Mitchell is back, panting a little.

"Why'd you park way back there?"

"I didn't want to take a chance that somebody would scratch our car with their door."

"Our car?"

"Oh, I just meant that we both use it."

"Yes, I know we do."

Charlie smiles and shakes her head. She is getting to like her new partner.

"What've you got?"

Mitchell hands Charlie the packet of crime scene seals, tape, and a cell phone.

"I've got a phone too. We can talk just by pressing this button on the side, see? It's just like the old war movies. Able one this is Able two. Isn't that cool?"

"Cool," answers Charlie, trying to figure out if she knows how to work this thing.

Mitchell continues. "You could be Able one, and I could be Able two. What do you think?"

"I'll tell you what, you be Mitchell and I'll be Charlie. Okay?"

Mitchell is caught up in his war movie. "Roger, Wilco, and Out."

Mitchell is excited, like a kid at Christmas. He pulls open his jacket. "And I've got this…and a holster too…and handcuffs. I'm ready to roll."

Charlie is shocked when she sees the gun. It's huge! A .44 caliber S&W Magnum. Just like Dirty Harry in the movies. Mitchell starts to take out the gun, but Charlie stops him.

"No, no. That's okay, I'll see it later. We've got a lot to do. What did they find about the blood?"

"Oh, I almost forgot. It was Fairall's blood okay."

"That means the murder happened back there, under the Ferris wheel," she mumbles. "Let's get something to eat."

"I thought you'd never ask. I'm starving."

"Wait a minute," Charlie orders, "did you get the laptop?"

"Oh yeah." Mitchell looks around like he's lost something. "Oh yeah, I left it in the car. Be right back." Mitchell heads for the Volkswagen and Charlie heads for Carrie's Restaurant.

She stands outside the restaurant, waiting for Mitchell, and reviewing things in her mind. *So Fairall got whacked under the Ferris wheel.*

Mitchell runs up and hands Charlie the laptop. She takes a quick look at it and hands it back. "You can be in charge of that."

Carrie's Restaurant – Tuesday, 6/22 – 1340 hrs.

There are eight or ten people eating; a couple of guys at the counter and the rest scattered around the tables. Charlie is surprised to see this many people. Putting the tape on the gate didn't seem to be working. But, like Barker said, people come to eat, not for the rides. They know where the service entrance is located.

"Did you see anyone come in the park?"

Mitchell shakes his head no. Carrie spots them and points for Charlie to take the table in the corner. They do. Mitchell studies the menu.

"I'm starved."

Charlie hasn't looked at the menu. She is still checking out the key ring.

"This one looks like a house key. It's stamped WCAP. I wonder what that means."

Mitchell smiles and jumps around like a kid who knows the answer to the teacher's question. "I know...I know...WCAP—Walnut Creek Amusement Park."

"Hey, very good. I'll bet Fairall lost these. Did he have anything else in his pockets?"

"I don't know, and I'm not going back to check," says Mitchell.

"We should have checked when we visited the morgue. I want you to call the M.E. and find out."

"What's an M.E.?"

"M.E., Medical Examiner."

"Oh I get it, Doctor Kidwell."

Charlie nods and looks around the room. She notices two young college-aged girls waiting tables. She knew Carrie could do it all by herself. She's in good shape, no spring chicken.

Carrie stops by the table to take their order. She looks at Charlie and waits.

"I'll have a grilled cheese and a diet soda."

Carrie nods to Mitchell.

"And you?"

I'll have your double cheeseburger, fries—supersize those fries…and a chocolate milk shake. What kind of pie do you have?"

"You have a big appetite for such a small man. I just took the apple pie out of the oven."

"That's great! I'll have that."

"It'll take a minute," says Carrie and she leaves.

As Mitchell and Charlie wait, she gives him instructions; he takes notes.

"After you call the M.E. about Fairall's pockets, get the phone records for this place, the business phone. Find out if Fairall or Barker had cell phones. Get those records too. Check both of them for a rap sheet—including traffic stuff. Maybe you can do that on the laptop."

In what seems like only a few minutes, Carrie returns with the food. It looks wonderful, and Mitchell digs in. Charlie takes a bite of her grilled cheese sandwich. It's delicious.

"How can one cheese sandwich be better than another? I've never tasted anything this good. How's you burger?"

Mitchell's mouth is so full he can't answer. He nods, points to his mouth, and makes a humming noise.

"I'll take that for 'good.'"

When they finish their lunch Charlie walks to the cash register. She doesn't have a guest check. Carrie is standing at the counter sorting out bills.

Carrie shakes her head in a motioning gesture. "Over there," she whispers. "The big guy—over there—at the counter. One of Fairall's friends."

"I'll check it out," says Charlie.

Charlie looks over in the direction of the counter. It's the big black guy that was talking with the dwarf.

Charlie puts away as much information as she can see. *Big guy, black, forty-five or fifty, maybe two fifty, two sixty pounds, ugly, mean looking, long nasty scar on cheek, White Sox ball cap, Nike shoes, expensive.*

Carrie's face sours. She doesn't like that idea.

Charlie gives Mitchell a high sign to back her up. She walks by the guy and takes a seat, two seats away. She studies the menu.

The big guy gives Charlie the once-over. "Hello, miss," he says in a soft voice. "You gonna have lunch?"

Charlie smiles. "No, I've already eaten—grilled cheese sandwich—delicious—you should try it." She points to the menu. "I was thinking about having some pie."

He nods. "Don't spoil that girly figure. You work around here?"

"No, I'm looking for somebody. Do you know a man named Fairall?"

"Wild Bill Fairall? Yeah, I knew him, what about it?"

"I'm looking for him. Somebody told me he could help me with my..." she lowers her voice, "...my uh, problem."

The big guy squints his eyes and looks at Charlie.

"What kind of a problem is that?" he asks.

Charlie glances around the room to see if anyone is watching or can hear."

"I better not talk about it. It's kind of personal."

Now, the black guy glances around the room.

Does it have anything to do with..." his voice goes into a whisper, "a white powder?"

Charlie acts shocked. "You a cop?" she asks.

"Are you kidding? Do I look like a cop?"

Charlie shrugs her shoulders.

"Maybe I can help you with your...uh, problem. Fairall worked for me. I'm the guy who delivers to him."

He takes another look around. "I can give you a better deal than he could. And, if you have any rich little girl friends, you can help them, get *your* stuff free."

Charlie's blown away! She didn't expect this kind of response. She sits quiet, wondering what to do.

She turns to the face the man. "What do they call you?"

He doesn't hesitate at all. "They call me RT."

"Arty?" asks Charlie. "That's an unusual name for an African-American."

59

"No, not Arty, RT. I'm from Alabama, down there sometimes people call you by your initials. Mine are R and T so they call me RT, not Arty. Anyway, I'm not an African-American, I'm from Alabama. I'm an Alabama-American."

Charlie's feeling confident. She chuckles. "I've got to check some stuff out, RT, how can I get hold of you? You got a number?"

"Yeah," he says, taking a napkin from the holder. He slips a pen from his shirt pocket and writes a number on the napkin. Looking around, he shoves the napkin toward Charlie.

She picks up the napkin, reads it, and puts it inside her side pocket.

She jumps up and says, "I gotta go now." She holds up her hand with thumb and little finger extended and put her hand up to her ear. "I'll call you," and she walks to the cash register. RT returns to his coffee. Charlie is shaking.

Carrie is standing at the cash register. She gestures toward RT, rolls her eyes, and mouths the word *Wow*.

"What's the damage?" asks Charlie.

"Oh no. This one's on the house."

Charlie puts down a twenty. In almost a whisper, so RT can't hear, she says, "No offense, but it wouldn't be right for us to accept a meal while we're working. We have to live by our code of ethics or we can't honestly serve the people."

"I'm impressed," says Carrie, and also in a whisper, "You're exactly right and it was foolish for me to put you in that spot."

She punches key and turns the crank. "That'll be twelve forty-two."

Charlie pushes back a couple of singles and says, "Tip that waitress; she did a wonderful job."

Carrie chuckles. "See you for dinner?"

"Maybe. Maybe lunch again, tomorrow."

She grabs Mitchell by the arm and ushers him out.

Outside Carrie's Restaurant – Tuesday, 6/22 – 1520 hrs.

Outside, Charlie looks at the WCAP key. "That was scary stuff. I don't want to get closer to that creep. I'm going to give this napkin to the Narcs, but let's add him to our suspect list anyway. He referred to Fairall in the past tense, so he knows he's dead. I think he wants to take over Fairall's drug business. He could be our guy."

"Fairall was a drug dealer?"

"RT told me he was the one who supplied Fairall. What else could he be? Fairall had to be a big time dealer."

"What are we going to do about this guy? The RT guy?" asks Mitchell.

"I'm not going to do anything now. We'll give this napkin and his description to the Narcs and they can handle it. If he turns out to be our guy, we'll know where to find him."

Mitchell nods his understanding.

Charlie looks at the WCAP key.

"This has to be for the restaurant or that circus wagon," she says out loud.

She thinks for a few seconds and heads for the circus wagon.

Mitchell and Charlie stand, looking at the circus wagon.

Mitchell says, "I think I'll look around for more clues." Charlie nods her permission, and Mitchell wanders off toward the rides.

The Circus Wagon – Tuesday, 6/22 – 1542 hrs.

She's tempted to knock, but decides to try the key. First, she checks out the outside of the wagon. In its own way, it's beautiful, and in wonderful condition. Even the wheels are decorated. She climbs up the wooden steps and slips the key in the slot. A quick turn and the door opens.

Barker is inside! He looks up. "Come on in."

He startles Charlie, but she shoves the door open and steps inside. Cigar smoke hits her right in the face. Her first reaction is that the wagon looked much bigger on the inside than one might expect it to look on the outside. She glances around. A large antique roll-top desk occupies the center of the room.

Everywhere she looks there are photographs and posters of circus people and the various performers who had worked for Fairall. Barker sits on a large old safe, smoking a cigar. A small oriental rug is spread in front of the desk. Charlie looks at it and says, "Wow, that's quite a rug. I'll bet it's worth a bundle."

Barker leans forward to see it. "I never noticed it. Bill bought lots of good stuff, so I wouldn't be surprised if was worth some money. I'll have to check it out now that it's mine. Want to buy it?"

"Not with those cigar ashes on top of it."

Barker quickly looks for someplace to knock the large ash from his cigar. He puts the ashes in his cupped hand and dumps them in the trash can.

"What's in the safe?"

Barker hops down and steps away. "Bill kept all the important papers and all the cash money in there. Every week I'd come over and he'd count out the bills to make the payroll. We pay in cash. I don't have the combination. Hafta get a locksmith, I guess."

"You pay in cash? What about taxes?"

Barker just shrugs and wrinkles up his nose like he smelled a bad smell. "What about 'em?"

Charlie steps up to the safe and studies the front. Like everything else, it's boldly decorated. She can't resist putting her hand on the big brass handle. She turns and pulls. The door swings open. Charlie is surprised; Barker is astonished.

"How'd you do that?" he asked. She doesn't answer.

"It's an art," Charlie cracks. "Let's look inside."

"Don't you need a warrant to do that?"

"Are all you people lawyers? That's up to you. Should I get a warrant?" Charlie used her best threatening voice. "I can do that, but my partner will have to guard the place till I get it."

"I guess you won't need one. Go ahead and look."

By the time the little question and answer period was over, Charlie was already on her knees, rooting around inside the safe. Standard stuff you would expect to find. The only interesting thing was a shoe box. Charlie opens it. The box is full of money! Jam-packed full of bills. She has never seen so much money. She turns to Barker with a questioning look.

"That's the cash for the payroll. Like I told you, he would dig into that shoe box and give me some cash for the payroll. I'd divide it up and give it to the performers. Here, give it to me and I'll get rid of it."

"I don't think so," says Charlie. "It's evidence now and I'll have to hold onto it."

Those were not the words Barker wanted to hear.

As Charlie puts the shoebox back into the safe, she notices a very small amount of white powder. Cocaine, she thinks, but she doesn't say anything to Barker.

"I'm going to declare this whole wagon a crime scene and seal it up."

Barker is instantly angry. "You can't do that!" he barked.

Calmly, Charlie offered a half smile and said, "Do we have to go through this again? Watch me! Until further notice, this place is off limits to everyone, including you. If I find somebody—anybody—in here, they're headed for the slammer for a long, long time. I'll have my partner put a seal on the door to make it official. You can leave now."

Barker moaned. "Leave? I've got business here."

"Not today you don't. Leave!"

Barker walks to the door. He turns to make one last appeal only to meet Charlie's stare. He decides to just go.

Just then, Charlie's cell phone vibrates in her pocket.

"Chandler," she says in her most professional voice.

"It's John Spencer, Charlie. How's it going?"

"Bit by bit," she answers.

"Your guy Mitchell was here. I gave him all the stuff he wanted. I also gave him a set of phones with walkie-talkie capability so you two can talk to teach other."

"I'm talking on it. You also gave him a small canon."

"It was all I could get. He'll be okay with it."

"I'd feel better if he spent a couple of days on the range getting qualified."

"Have him go to the range this Saturday. They open around noon on Saturday."

"I'm about to start more interviews with the—uh—performers. There's some strange stuff going on here."

"Okay. Maybe I'll stop out there later today; tomorrow for sure. Let me know if you need anything. The chief has been asking about you."

"Asking about me? How nice."

"See ya."

She hangs up.

Charlie takes one more look around; her eyes set to scan without knowing exactly what she is looking for. The safe. The posters. The Chair. The big desk. The oriental rug. Nothing, then suddenly she focuses on a business card laying in the very center of the desk. She had missed it. She picks it up and reads it. *James A. Miller, Real Estate Developer, Contractors, Builders. Offices in Columbus, Dayton, and Cincinnati.* She flips the card over. The addresses of the various offices are listed on the back. *Columbus Office: 2352 East Main Street, Bexley, Ohio 43209. (614) 555-2655*

"I gotta think," she says out loud.

She also wonders about that white powder in the safe. She'd have to take another look. There is something about the inside of that safe that bothers her, but she doesn't know exactly what it is. She's never seen a safe that huge. Should she count the money? She decides it wouldn't make any difference. She swings the big door closed, making sure not to close it tight and trip the lock. What's the connection with this Miller person?

Charlie presses the walkie-talkie button on her phone. "Mitchell?"

"This is Mitchell, over."

"I'm in the circus wagon, Mitchell. I've got something for you."

"This is Mitchell. Roger Wilco, and out."

She smiles and shakes her head as she puts the phone back in her pocket.

She opens the door, and Mitchell is standing there!

"I've been out here, waiting."

"Put a seal on that door."

Mitchell hands Charlie the laptop and runs to the front of the wagon.

She holds the little computer up to examine it.

"Hmmmm, Not bad. This could come in handy."

Mitchell plasters a *CRIME SCENE Do Not Enter* sticker on the door. He turns to leave, but stops at the bottom of the stairs and looks back to admire his handiwork. *That's not going to keep anyone out*, he thinks. He scampers back up the steps and puts another sticker on the door. This time part of the seal is on the door, and part on the door jam. "Ahhh, that is the right way," he tells himself.

Charlie checks her watch. "You ever been to Columbus?" she ask Mitchell.

"Yeah, sure, lots of times."

"I'm going to take a run up there, want to go?"

"Gee, I can't. I promised my mom that I'd fix the TV dish tonight."

"Okay, I'm going to run up to Columbus and see this Miller guy. You can call a cab...put it on you expense account."

"Expense account?" Mitchell wonders. "Do I have an expense account?"

"Get a receipt," Charlie warns.

When they reach Charlie's Volkswagen they get a shock. The tires are flat! All four tires are completely flat!

"Oh, God! What's this all about? We're stuck. What now?"

Mitchell just looks.

"Let's get Fred, that maintenance character. Run down and see if you can find him. See if he can help us with his magic two-wheeled work bench."

Mitchell takes off running. Charlie looks at her tires.

In just a few minutes, Fred Doer and Mitchell show up.

"Gotta problem, miss?" Fred asks.

"You bet," Charlie answers. "I've got four of them; four flat tires. Can you the help us?"

Fred Doer slowly walks around the car, spending a few seconds with each wheel."

"They're flat okay. But no problem, missy, the ol' Kearsarge will have those tires pumped in no time, and you'll be on your way."

Fred pulls the cart up close to the car. He fiddles around the front and starts a small generator. Charlie notices that it's amazingly quiet. Then, he swings open the back door and start pulling out a red hose. The compressor is running inside. Fred skips around the car filling each tire and checking the pressure with the gage he keeps in his pocket. He's actually whistling, "Whistle While You work."

Charlie steps up next to Mitchell. "Isn't he darling?" she says.

"Yeah," Mitchell says, "darling." He rolls his eyes.

Fred finishes the job and stands wiping his hands on a towel, waiting for word of approval and gratitude.

"Fred, I can't tell you how much I appreciate your help. We would have been goners without you and the USS Kearsarge."

Fred does a complete "aw shucks" routine, head down, rocking, looking down at his shoes. Charlie can't resist. She gives him a kiss on the cheek, and Fred is speechless.

Mitchell steps up. "Hey, Fred, did you know that one of the wheels is missing on that kiddy-car ride? The silver car."

Fred frowns. "I sure do, mister. That's not all. I've been trying to get Fairall to order parts for the last couple of months. I need more than that little wheel. He just let my work orders pile up on his desk." He just shakes his head. Mitchell has hit a hot button.

"Well, I have to go," says Fred, and turns his cart and walks away, mumbling to himself.

"We have to figure out who did this, Mitchell. Somebody's causing trouble."

"Maybe they want to get rid of us."

"I don't see how anyone could think that. We're the police department. Even if they killed us, they have to know that more cops would show up. No, it's something else."

Charlie and Mitchell climb in the Volkswagen.

"I think this may have been a way to delay us," says Charlie. Mitchell nods his agreement.

"I'm going to take a run up to Columbus, but it's too late to go now. I'll take you over to headquarters, and take off in the morning. You come to the park tomorrow and poke around.

Office of James A. Miller – Wednesday, 6/23 – 0948 hrs.

The building was obviously a made-over gas station. Charlie remembers a building like that when she was a kid, riding around with her dad. It actually looks like a friendly little cottage. A peaked dormer over the front door, tall sloping blue-shingled roof. It's painted pure white, with green shutters. The large window in the front holds a sign. *James A. Miller, Real Estate Development, Contractors, Builders.*

She parks her bug right at the front door, ignoring the yellow lines to designate parking spaces. She jumps out and heads for the front door. A small sign says, *Walk In,* and she does. Just inside the door sits a secretary, or receptionist, or something...a woman about 25, nice hair, nice complexion, pretty face, good body, cheap perfume.

She looks up at Charlie and smiles. "May I help you?"

"I would like to see Mister Miller, please."

"Do you have an appointment?"

"Do I need one?"

"Yes, Mister Miller is very busy."

"Is he in the building?"

"Yes but..."

Charlie holds out her badge and stops the woman cold.

"Tell him I'd like to see him."

The woman grabs her telephone and presses a button on the consol. In just a few seconds, she says, "Mister Miller, the police are out here to see you."

Before she can replace the hand set, a door opens and a smiling man flies out the door and grabs Charlie's hand.

"Miller, Jim Miller. Nice to meet you, Officer...?" He continues to pump Charlie's hand.

"Chandler. Detective Chandler. Can we talk?"

He ushers Charlie into his office. For such a big, important man, he has a tiny office. The receptionist has a bigger office. Miller hurries around his rather ordinary desk, and motions Charlie to a straight-back chair in the corner. As she gets settled, she puts Miller into her witness file. *Maybe forty-five, fifty. Tall, six two or three, well built, two ten, two twenty. Nice looking, not handsome, but nice looking. Straight-back black hair, graying on the temples. Small bald spot on the back of his head. Very heavy wire rim designer glasses. Sharp dresser.*

"I have to apologize for the size of the office. As a developer, I spend most of my time in the field. I come here to make phone calls and check my mail. What can I do for you, Detective...uh...?"

"Chandler, Detective Charlie Chandler," and she digs right in. "I understand that you're interested in the Walnut Creek Amusement Park."

"Well, I'm not interested in the park; I'm interested in the property. It would make a wonderful housing development. I could put sixty very nice homes on that property. Turn it into something useful." He reaches behind his chair and pulls out a 30 X 40 artist's conception of his idea. Charlie is impressed. It would be better than all those junky rides and the side show.

"Are you talking with Mister Fairall about this...uh project?"

"Fairall? No, a guy named Barker is my contact, and he tells me that Fairall is dead."

"What do you know about Fairall?"

"Not much. I talked to him a couple of times and he wasn't interested in the project. Barker came to see me and told me he was half owner of the property, and could handle the deal."

"Then, you're going ahead with it?"

"Well, it was in limbo while Barker convinced Fairall to go ahead, but now there's no Fairall. To tell you the truth, I'm about ready to bail out."

"When was the last time you talked with Fairall?"

"Maybe two, three weeks ago."

Charlie stands up and puts out her hand. "Well, Mister Miller, I thank you for your time. If anything comes up, I trust that I can contact you. Here's my card."

Miller takes Charlie's card and reads it. Automatically, he fishes out one of his cards and hands it to her. "Good luck on your project," she says, and leaves.

As Charlie sits at the traffic light, she glances in her rearview mirror. An older Lincoln four-door pulls up in front of Miller's office. A very large black man gets out and walks to door. The light changes, but Charlie is nailed to the mirror. *Can that be RT?* she wonders. Charlie makes a right turn and heads for the next traffic light. There, she pops the red light on her roof and plugs it in. Traffic stops while she makes a U-turn right on Main Street. She speeds back and parks across the street from Miller's office. The Volkswagen doesn't give her much room, but she sinks down in the seat hoping to see without being seen.

What's the connection between Miller, RT and Fairall? she wonders. Fishing around in her mind for an answer, she waits and watches. She's set for a long stakeout, but it only lasts a few minutes. Before she can get settled, the office door swings open and both RT and Miller step out. They are obviously saying their goodbyes. RT has a large manila envelope under his arm. Miller puts one hand on RT's shoulder and they shake hands. *Boy, how friendly can it get? No kiss?* Charlie thinks.

RT is in his car and gone before Charlie can come up with a plan. She watches him disappear in the opposite direction down Main Street and knows that she can't possibly get turned around in time to follow him.

"Might as well go home," she mumbles.

Her mind switches away from RT and Miller. "I've got to think about things. I want to talk with the performers tomorrow," she says out loud. "That should be interesting."

But as she drives away, she can't help thinking, *What's the connection between Miller, RT, and Fairall?*

WCAP – Wednesday, 6/23 – 1220 hrs.

Charlie returns to the park, but where's Mitchell? She pulls up to the crest of the hill where she can survey the park. The rides, The Show Tent, The Fun House, Carrie's restaurant. The restaurant, of course! The restaurant!

She pulls up to the no parking zone and gets out. Before going in, she peeks in the big front window. There, sitting at the counter, is her partner eating pie.

Charlie walks in and take a seat next to Mitchell. He's startled.

"Okay if I join you?"

Mitchell, mouth full of pie, nods.

Carrie emerges from the kitchen. A big smile when she see Charlie. "What can I get for you, Charlie?"

"I'll have a piece of that wonderful apple pie and a cup of your also-wonderful coffee."

"Did you find anything in Columbus?" asks Mitchell.

"I'm not sure. Remember the black guy, RT?"

Mitchell nods, his mouth still full of pie.

"He has some connection with this guy Miller, who has a connection with Fairall and Barker. I wish I knew. Let's eat and start the questioning."

The Show Tent – Wednesday, 6/23 – 1232 hrs.

Mitchell and Charlie shove the tent flap aside and walk in the big tent. There are as many large hand-painted posters inside as there are outside. Again, each poster has a small stage in front of it, about four or five feet from the ground. During the show, a crowd of customers can move from one performer to the next.

Charlie doesn't know it, but each performer has living quarters behind their poster. Directly behind each poster is a wall with a door to the performer's apartment. The place has an eerie quietness to it. The detective and her sidekick stand silent, taking in the scene.

"This place is spooky," says Charlie.

"Spooky," echoes Mitchell. "Gives me the creeps."

A shot rings out!

Charlie flies backward and lands hard on the dirt floor. She lays there—motionless—spread eagle on her back. Mitchell is in shock. His mind races, but he doesn't know what to do.

He quickly looks around, but doesn't see anyone. He's afraid to be there; he's afraid to leave. He kneels next to Charlie. Her eyes are closed. "My God, she's dead," he says out loud to himself. He moves to cover her with his body and remembers his gun. The huge gun comes out and in a jerky motion he points it around the room, scanning for the shooter.

Charlie moans.

"Oh God! You're alive." He tells himself, "Call 911," and he does.

"What is your emergency?" asks the operator.

"Officer down! Officer down!" yells Mitchell. "We need help at the Walnut Creek Amusement Park. Have an ambulance come to the Show Tent."

"I have someone on the way. Please hold on in case I have to talk with you."

"Okay, okay, I'll hold."

Mitchell looks at Charlie. There is a hole in her blouse smack dab in the center of her chest. She moans again. Mitchell is bouncing on his knees. "Come on, come on, come on."

He hears a commotion and looks to the tent flap for the emergency crew.

Charlie opens her eyes. Mitchell gets close to her face.

"Are you okay?"

Charlie gives a couple small shakes of her head as if to shake something off. She tries to speak. "What happened?"

"You got shot. Are you okay?"

"Shot?"

Charlie's hand moves to the hole in her blouse. She looks at her fingers. "No blood," she mumbles.

"Like Amos and Andy?" says Mitchell, trying to make the best of things.

Just then the ambulance arrives. Charlie slowly rolls over.

"Give me a hand up."

"Up?" asks Mitchell.

"Up!"

He takes her arm and helps Charlie gets up on her knees. Then she climbs up using Mitchell's small frame for support. Mitchell is speechless. A tear rolls down his cheek.

The emergency crew wheels in a gurney. "Where's the problem?" asks one of the responders.

Charlie is standing up. She's shaken, but in control. The guy with the gurney takes one look at Charlie. He spots the hole in her blouse and signals for a female assistant. Help comes from a very large woman, not one you would argue with. She forces Charlie to lay down on the gurney and checks her out for wounds. Mitchell stands at a respectful distance.

"You're one lucky lady," the technician tells Charlie.

Charlie is regaining her strength, feeling better, but is still confused. "What happened?" she asks.

The technician holds up the medallion. The chain is still around Charlie's neck. It looks like this medal kept a bullet out of your chest. Look at that dent.

Charlie grabs the medallion. She can't think of anything to say.

The ambulance driver steps up. "We're going to take you in for a check-up, ma'am."

"No, that won't be necessary. I'm okay now. It didn't even break the skin. I'll be fine, just fine."

Charlie climbs off the gurney. She brushes off her trousers.

Mitchell spots a folding chair leaning against the wall, and grabs it for Charlie. She's glad to sit down. She runs her fingers over her chest. There is a little pain, but it doesn't really bother her. "Crazy," she says.

Reluctantly, the emergency crew packs up their stuff, puts the gurney back in the ambulance and they drive off.

Charlie motions for Mitchell to come over.

"Thanks, Mitchell, you did a great job of taking care of me."

Mitchell is almost in tears.

"Did you see anyone?"

Mitchell shakes his head.

"I think the bad guy wants us to leave. Let's knock off for the day and pick up this mess in the morning. I've got to get my clothes cleaned and buy a new blouse. We'll get the bad guy tomorrow. Right now, I want you to set up a camera to watch that circus wagon door. I want it on all night."

Charlie turns to Charlie Chan. "Mouse only play when cat is believed to be asleep—*Charlie Chan at the Wax Museum.*"

"All night? I have to stay out here all night?"

"No, we'll need a real movie camera in a surveillance van."

"Where do I get a surveillance van?"

"You're a cop. You're on a case. You can order a van out here and they can set it up to tape all night. They have the big movie camera."

"Wow! I can do that?"

"You can do that. Come on, I'll give you a lift to the station and you can see about that van. I'm going home."

The little yellow car drives past the gate without a red light flashing and without waking up the wrinkled old man.

Charlie's House – Wednesday, 6/23 – 1915 hrs.

Mom puts the bowl of mashed potatoes in front of Charlie.

"I'll tell you, Charlie, I'm very upset about this shooting business. You could have been killed, and all for a bunch of carnival people."

Charlie helps herself to a couple of spoons full of potatoes. "I could get hit by a Greyhound bus."

Mom grits her teeth. "You know very well what I'm talking about. I'm your mother. Mothers worry."

Charlie fingers her medallion. "I've got this…It did its job today."

The phone rings.

Charlie jumps up. "Got it!"

She picks up the old candlestick style telephone. She holds the mouthpiece in one hand, ear piece in the other. "Hello?"

"Charlie, this is John Spencer. I'm sorry to bother you at home, but the chief wants to talk with you in the morning, before you head for the carnival. You need to turn in a significant incident report. Standard procedure."

"Okay, I can do that. I'll be there at eight."

"Great. How are you feeling?"

"I'm 100%. Very lucky."

73

"Mitchell told me what happened. Well, okay, see you in the morning."

"Wait! Will you do something for me?"

"Sure."

"Round up a couple dozen DNA swab kits. I may need them. I'll pick them up tomorrow."

"Done."

Click.

Charlie looks at the old phone. "Mom, why can't we get a modern phone? This is an antique."

"It's been around longer than you, Charlie. Actually we have another one even older. It was your grandpa's. It doesn't have a dial, so your dad found this one at a flea market. Grandpa's phone number was 74. Can you believe that, 74. You picked up the phone and the operator would say, "Operator." Then, all you had to do was say seven four. Anyway, I like it. It reminds me of some good times. It's like your dad had in his house when he was a kid. He liked it too."

Charlie smiles at that; she likes stories about her dad and grandpa. She pats the phone and says, "Good phone," and she sits down to finish her dinner.

Fadler's Office – Thursday, 6/24 – 0800 hrs.

Whatever you might say about George Fadler, he was a worker. At least, he put in the hours. He was always at his desk at seven A.M., and didn't leave until five. Sometimes he had a two-martini lunch, but that was only when the big boss invited him out, and paid for the lunch.

At eight A.M., Charlie, Mitchell, and John Spencer are standing outside Fadler's office door. He waves them in. Without being told, they line up by rank in front of the desk…like soldiers. John, then Charlie, then Mitchell.

"How are you feeling, Charlie?" Fadler asked.

"Fine, sir. I've got a championship bruise, but otherwise I'm fine."

"Good, I was worried about you. Can't have my new detective on the sick list. Is this your new partner?"

"Yes, sir, Mitchell Yen."

Fadler extends his hand. "Welcome aboard, Mitchell."

John can't believe his ears. Could it be that the old bird was going soft?

Fadler looks at Charlie. "You need to file an S.I.R."

"S.I.R., sir?"

"Significant Incident Report. The department likes to keep track of things that happen to our officers."

"Yes, sir."

"By the way, I've assigned a new car to you. The dealer delivered it this morning and it should be outside waiting for you. It's fully equipped, but unmarked. No sense running your own car on police business." With that, Fadler waves his hand, and everyone leaves.

"Boy, I've never seen him act like that," says John. "Let's hope this is a new Fadler." John hands the car keys to Charlie. "Black caddy SUV. Parked alongside the building, city tags."

Charlie bounces the keys in her hand. "We gotta go now; the show must go on."

Charlie and Mitchell start to leave when John calls out, "Don't forget your DNA kits. I had to call in a favor to get them. The CSI people protect their turf."

He turns to leave, but turns back and points to a laptop computer on his desk.

"Oh yeah, the computer. Do you both need one? Take it with you. You can e-mail activity reports and requests for help. I can e-mail you too, so check it when you boot up."

"One will do the job. Mitchell's black-belt on the computer." Charlie looks at Mitchell and he nods his agreement.

"Oh, John?"

John Spencer puts his head back in Fadler's office. "Yes, sir?"

"Could you step in for a minute?"

John wonders what's going on. Fadler never, ever calls him John. Step in here a minute? What's this about? John walks into the office.

Fadler pulls his big, fat frame out of the chair and meets John. He takes John's arm and speaks in a soft tone. "You gotta keep your eye

75

on the Amusement park thing and help Chandler. This case has attracted the attention of all the big shots. It seems that that Fairall character was a big time contributor to the political campaigns of several of our bosses. These guys are all over me."

John is uncomfortable with Fadler holding his arm. Gently, he breaks free. "Yes, sir. I'll watch Chandler's e-mails, and take a run out their every day or so."

"Every day," says the chief. "If she screws this thing up, dump her."

"Yes, sir," says John as he leaves the office, "every day." He thinks, *Fadler hasn't changed after all.*

WCAP – Thursday, 6/24 – 0936 hrs.

The new car rolls right by the guard shack and the old guy doesn't even look up. Mitchell is driving.

"Should we check him out? Maybe somebody whacked him too," says Mitchell.

"We've got enough going on."

Mitchell pulls the car right up to the circus wagon. They both get out. Charlie sorts through the keys. *What was the thing? WCPA? CPWA? WCAP?*

"WCAP," says Mitchell. "Walnut Creek Amusement Park. Got it."

Circus Wagon – Thursday, 6/24 – 0950 hrs.

The evidence van with the camera is still parked near the wagon.

Charlie pulls off the seal and puts the key in the lock. She half expects Barker to be sitting there. She pushes the door open and hit the light switch.

"We've got some stuff to put in the evidence locker," she tells Mitchell.

She goes right to the safe, swings open the door and peers in. The box of money is gone! Charlie is amazed; confused; surprised; dumfounded.

"Impossible! How could this be?" She looks at the door. The seal is still on the door. "How could someone get in here and swipe that money?"

Mitchell just stands there, mouth open. He feels like he should say something, but he doesn't have an answer. "Now our case has murder, drugs, and theft. We're going to be busy."

Once again, Charlie calls on Charlie Chan. "Dog cannot chase three rabbits at same time."

"Let's get in that van and check the tape."

Mitchell says, "Charlie...we have a problem. The camera has been running about ten hours, right. It's real time, right?"

Charlie grows impatient. "What is it, Mitchell?"

"If it took ten hours to make the tape, it'll take us at least ten hours to watch it."

Charlie slaps her forehead. "Dumb Ass!" She thinks a few seconds. "Maybe we can put it on fast forward or something," says Charlie.

Mitchell shrugs. "I don't know how it works."

They try the back door of the van. It's locked. Of course, they aren't going to leave the thing unlocked. Someone could turn off the camera, or even steal the van.

"Call the CSI people and ask them to come out and help us look at the tape. Say please."

Mitchell walks to the wagon and sits down on the steps. He pulls out his new phone and starts punching buttons.

Charlie shakes her head. *Stupid, stupid, stupid! Charlie Chandler, the great female detective. I would have done better to bring a lawn chair and a sleeping bag. I wonder what Charlie Can would do.*

Show Tent – Friday, 6/25 – 1020 hrs.

She walks to the show tent and pulls the flap back. She's a little uneasy about going in, what with the shot and all. She calls out, "Barker. Barker, you in there?"

As if on cue, Barker steps out from behind one of the Fat Man's posters. He knew that she was there.

The poster says the fat man weights eighteen hundred pounds! Barker jumps down off the stage.

"Visiting with Pete. How you feeling?"

"I'm okay."

"That was a hell of a thing that happened to you yesterday. I can't explain it. Do you have any ideas?"

"Not a one. Do you have surveillance cameras? " asks Charlie, thinking that maybe it was Barker who shot her.

"Surveillance cameras? Who do you think we are, Barnum and Bailey?"

"Very funny. I want to start interviewing people now. We still have a murder to solve."

"Sure, where do we start?"

"*WE* don't start anyplace. I start—you stand outside and be quiet—I'll do the police work. There's no plan, so let's just start with the first guy and work my way around. Who's first?"

"The fat man is in apartment number one. We...uh, you can start there. Come on."

Barker climbs up on the stage and offers Charlie a hand up. She takes his hand and he pulls her up. She studies the poster showing a huge man sitting on a bed.

"Does he really weight eighteen hundred pounds?"

"Actually, it's more like eight, but that's plenty. He's a nice guy. He likes to talk with people, and they like to talk with him."

"How do they talk to him if he's in bed all the time?"

Barker's chest swells in pride. "I invented an ingenious gadget to do that. The front of his apartment is like a garage door...it opens all the way. We pull the poster aside like a shower curtain, and the door goes up! But, that ain't all. Pete's bed slides out like magic so he's close to the people. Sometimes he wears a throat mike. How about that?"

Charlie is generally impressed. "How about that! I have to admit, it's *very* clever," she says, slowly nodding her head.

Barker shines in all his glory. He knocks on the door. "Pete…you in there? Can we come in?"

"Come on in," a husky voice replies.

Charlie and Barker walk in the tiny apartment. It's not much wider than the poster, maybe twelve feet, and it's about thirty feet long. Wall to wall carpet, light brown. Framed circus posters on the walls.

The far end has three casement windows with a very nice view of Walnut Creek and of the woods. It's sparsely furnished, but then the fat man never leaves his bed. He doesn't need much in the way of furniture.

"Bart, why do you ask if I'm in here? I'm always in here." He smiles at Charlie. "Are you the police lady who got shot?"

"Yeah, that's me. My name is Detective Charlie Chandler. Pete…can I call you Pete?"

The fat man smiles. "Please do."

Charlie turns back to face Barker and points to the door. "Out!" He offers a weak smile and walks out the door.

"Pete, do you have any idea why someone would kill Mr. Fairall?"

"Sex, money, or drugs. That's about it. That's what I see on TV."

"Do you have any ideas about who could have done it?"

"I'd love to help you, darling, but I haven't been out of this bed for four years, except to go to Florida in the winter."

Charlie doesn't know what to say.

"How do you take care of yourself? How to you cook and things?"

She wanted to ask how he went to the bathroom, but couldn't handle it.

"Wilma takes good care of me. She's the tattoo lady. Or at least she was the tattoo lady. Everybody's got tattoos now, so she doesn't perform any longer."

"Would you mind giving us a DNA sample?"

"I think it would be exciting. Sign me up."

Charlie opens the tube and takes out the swab.

"Open your mouth and I'll take a sample."

The fat man opens his mouth, but Charlie can't reach it, he's too big. She has to climb on the bed and lean on the man. *This is weird,* she thinks. But she gets her sample, and gets back on her feet. She puts the swab in the tube and caps it. She writes "Fat Man" to identify the sample.

"Thanks," says Charlie. "How about Wilma? Is she around? I'd like to talk with her and get a sample."

"Sure," and he calls out, "Wilma?"

She appears like magic. She's a pleasant looking woman, average height; average build, nice looking, but every square inch of her body—except her face—is covered with tattoos.

Charlie offers her hand. "Hello, Wilma, I'm Charlie Chandler. I'm the detective assigned to solve Mister Fairall's murder."

"How nice to meet you, Detective."

"Wilma," asks Charlie, "why do you think anyone would kill Mister Fairall?"

Wilma thinks for a long time. She looks around for Barker. He's just outside the door, and she knows that he can hear. "I can't think of any reason…or anybody off hand. We all get along pretty good here. He always took good care of us, so I don't think any of the performers would hurt him. Maybe it was an accident."

"Maybe…Wilma, would you mind if I took a DNA sample?"

"Wow, just like on TV. What do you want me to do?"

"Just open up."

She does, and Charlie runs the swab inside her mouth, then puts the swab in the tube. She labels it "tattooed lady."

"Okay, that does it. We'll be leaving now, Pete, Wilma. Thanks for all your help and the DNA sample."

"That's okay, I enjoyed the attention. Show business has been slow lately, and I don't get a chance to talk with anybody."

Just as Charlie reaches the door, she turns back to the fat man. "Do you have a gun?" she asks.

He just smiles.

"Wilma?"

She shakes her head.

"Any idea who took a shot at me?"

Two heads shake no.

With that, Charlie gives a weak wave and walks out.

Barker is waiting outside. Charlie says, "Nice guy, who's next?"

"Let's try the snake lady."

"Ooooh, the snake lady," Charlie says under her breath.

They move to the second apartment, and Barker knocks.

"You home, Miss Clara?"

"Yes, come on in. I've been waiting for you"

Charlie steps into another world. Snakes everywhere; real and rubber. Small palm trees, plants, and an aquarium full of tropical fish. It seems hot, and feels humid. An iguana lizard hangs from a plastic palm tree. This must be what the Amazon jungle is like. Miss Clara, the snake lady, sits in a high-back bamboo chair with a huge snake wrapped around her neck.

"I know why you're here, dear. I'd love to give you a DNA sample. What do I do?"

"Just open your mouth and I'll put this swab inside to collect a sample. It's quite easy."

"Go ahead," the snake lady says and she sits there like a baby bird, with her mouth wide open.

Charlie fishes out the DNA kit and moves closer. The giant snake raises its head. It looks right at her, tongue whipping in and out. Charlie's hand trembles.

"He's not going to bite me…is he?"

"He's a she, and no she won't bite you. She's as gentle as a kitten."

Charlie thinks, *I'll bet she'd like to have a kitten for lunch.* She takes the DNA sample, puts the swab in the tube and identifies it as "Snake Lady."

"A couple of questions if you don't mind."

Miss Clara waves Charlie to a nearby seat.

"Go," says the snake lady.

Before Charlie can get her first question out, she feels something on her shoulder. She's startled, but keeps her composure. Whatever it is has sharp claws and it breathes heavy. Mentally, she eliminates a snake, and decides that it is a cat.

"Do you have any idea who killed Mr. Fairall?"

"I sure do. It was that nasty little midget who runs the Ferris wheel."

Charlie is surprised. This is the first time that anyone has accused anyone of anything.

She put a hand on her shoulder to remove the kitten, only to find that it's not a kitten. A tiny hand grabs her finger. It's a monkey! Charlie's heart leaps.

"Now you behave yourself, you little stinker," the snake lady tells the monkey.

"Does he bite?"

"No, he's a good boy. He just wants to snuggle with you and check out your jewelry. Make sure you check your earrings when you leave. He's a little kleptomaniac. Sometimes he can be sneaky."

"What makes you think the midget killed Mister Fairall?"

"He tried to steal one of my snakes; said he was going to eat it. Anybody who would eat a snake would kill a person."

"Okay, let me ask another question. Do you have a gun?"

"As a matter of fact, I do."

Charlie is genuinely surprised. "May I see it?"

"It's in that drawer over there. Help yourself."

Charlie opens the drawer and takes out the gun. It's a little two-shot derringer, a lady's gun; twenty five caliber. She holds it up to here nose and sniffs to see if it's been fired. It hasn't.

The snake lady laughs and says, "Honey, nobody has fired that gun in 25 years. It doesn't even work anymore. It's harmless."

Charlie gently puts the gun back in the drawer. "I'd advise you to get rid of that gun. It's always the empty gun or the broken gun that kills somebody."

The snake lady sees that she is serious. "You take the gun now and get rid of it for me. Will you?"

Charlie nods, picks up the gun. She makes certain that it's empty and puts the gun and the two bullets in her pocket. "I'll take care of it for you."

Charlie starts for the door. The monkey jumps off and lands on a nearby bookcase. Charlie checks her earrings. They're there.

"Wait a minute," says the snake lady. "I have something for you."
She reaches into a box near her chair and brings out a snake! She holds it out for Charlie.

"Oh no, I couldn't possibly take one of your snakes." She cringes at the thought. "Thanks anyway."

"It's rubber," laughs the snake lady. "Doesn't it look real?"

"Yeah, real." Charlie doesn't want to hurt her feelings. "I'll take it, and I thank you very much."

She and Barker leave.

Outside, Mitchell Yen is waiting. Charlie tosses the rubber snake to him. He screams and jumps right off the stage, batting the snake away. Then, realizing that the snake is rubber, he climbs back up on the stage, snake in hand. He feels foolish, and Charlie realizes it was a dumb thing to do.

"I'm sorry, Mitchell, I should know better."

"How could a rubber snake look that real?" asks Mitchell.

Charlie draws on Charlie Chan once more: "Cotton candy not made of cotton."

Mitchell laughs. "You know? It *was* kind of funny. Can I keep it?"

She nods, then gets Barker's attention. "Okay, who's next?"

Barker says, "The magician—The Great Crozboney."

Under her breath, *Really! The Great Crozboney. This place is beyond weird. Why am I not surprised?*

Barker bangs on the door. "Croz, you in there?"

There is a long silence and then a very low eerie music starts. Barker bangs on the door again.

"Croz, we need to talk to you."

The music becomes louder. The door slowly creeks open, revealing a pitch black room. A voice that sounds like it's coming from a speaker says, "Welcome to the world of The Great Crozboney."

Barker shrugs his shoulders and gives Charlie an apologetic look. "Show business."

Barker steps into the darkness. "Croz, the police are here. The police are here. They want to talk about Wild Bill."

A tiny beam of light appears on the floor, and then it grows and grows to show The Great Crozboney. He is dressed in a tuxedo, complete with top hat, a cap, and a walking stick. Charlie's mouth hangs open.

Slowly, the room light comes up. The Great Crozboney steps forward. In a flash, his walking stick turns into a bouquet of flowers. He tosses the flowers aside, and holds out a deck of cards.

"Take a card—any card."

"Mister, uh, Crozboney, we're here to talk about Mister Fairall's murder."

Crozboney shoves the deck of cards closer to Charlie.

"Take a card! Any card."

Charlie rolls her eyes and takes a card.

"Write your name on the card and place it back in the deck."

Charlie complies and stands there. She takes a deep breath and looks at her watch. *What's going on here?* she asks herself.

"Is this going to take long?"

Crozboney ignores the question and continues with his act.

"I will now find your card."

He turns away from Charlie. In a lightning fast move, he tosses the deck in the air, pulls a gun, and shoots at the flying cards!

When he turns back both Charlie and Mitchell have their guns out and pointing at him. He's terrified and drops his gun.

Charlie nods to Mitchell. "Cuff him."

Crozboney doesn't say a word. Mitchell springs into action and whips out his new handcuffs. In just seconds, the magician is handcuffed. Mitchell spins him around facing Charlie.

Charlie smiles at Mitchell. "That was excellent!"

Mitchell proudly says. "First in my class at the academy."

The Great Crozboney brings his right hand out from behind him. The handcuffs hang from his wrist, one cuff open. Without saying a word, he swings his other arm around. He places his free hand over the cuff on this wrist, and it seems to spring open at his touch. He hands the cuffs to Mitchell. "Good job, Officer, well done. Now, what can I do to help?"

Guns are still out. Charlie side-steps over to the magician's gun on the floor. Without taking her eyes off him, she stoops and picks up the gun. She looks at it and hands it off to Mitchell.

Without taking his eye off the magician, gun still drawn, he places the gun in his side pocket. "I'll send it in for ballistics this afternoon."

"Don't bother," says Charlie. "It's a blank gun."

"Blank?"

Charlie puts her gun in its holster.

"Okay, mister magician man, you ready to answer questions?"

Crozboney presses his index finger to his lips. "Shhhhh."

He steps to the scattered cards on the floor. He bends down and picks up one card, and hands it to Charlie. The card has her name on it, and there is a bullet hole right in the center.

"Your card?"

She's puzzled. She takes the card, but she's had enough.

"Where were you the night before last?"

"Here."

'Where were you last night?"

"Here...I'm always here. This kind of work demands a lot of practice."

"What kind of a man was Fairall?"

"Oh he was a very good man, very good. He helped me get out of the gutter and get back to my first love—magic. A wonderful man."

"Why would anyone kill him?"

The magician's head drops. "I don't know. It's so sad."

Charlie decides that she's wasting her time with this guy. He's harmless.

"If you were going to make a box disappear, how would you do it?"

"How big is the box, where is the box, and where do you want it to disappear to?"

"A shoe box."

The magician thinks for a few seconds.

"Let me think...how I can tell you so it makes sense to a non-magician," as if he's talking about a lower class of people.

He starts nodding his head. "How's this: Magic is not magic. There's no real magic, just illusions and slight of hand. Only tricks. Most tricks are based on doing the unexpected. Your mind knows what should happen, so it's easy to trick you. Misdirection and slight of hand is the secret. I'd direct your attention to something other than the box, then I'd do something with the box. If I wanted to pick your pocket or put something in your pocket, I might bump you to direct your attention, and then I'd make a grab. For something big like a shoe box, I might have a secret compartment someplace; it has to go someplace. I'd stick the box in there while I have you doing whatever I told you to do. Does that help?"

"I'm not sure. How'd you do the hole in the card thing?" asks Charlie.

The magician just smiles.

"I need a DNA sample," demands Charlie, taking out a new tube.

"You already have it," says the magician. He points to her breast pocket. Charlie looks down at her pocket. Jammed in with her badge, a DNA tube sticks out. She shakes her head slowly. Her expression tells it all. She's ticked off.

"Enough with the tricks. I'll take the sample myself."

Mitchell hands her a new tube.

"Don't say a word," she tells the magician. "Open up," and she swabs his mouth. She writes "magician" on the label and hands the tube to Mitchell.

She reaches in her breast pocket and takes out the tube the magician somehow put there. She walks to a nearby waste can, breaks the tube on the edge of the can, and tosses it in. She turns to the magician.

"You could go to jail for interfering with a police investigation. Think about it!"

The Great Crozboney throws his cape up over his face so only his heavily made-up eyes peek out.

Charlie gives Mitchell a nod.

"Put your gun away, we're finished here."

Mitchell is startled. As if waking up from a deep sleep, he fumbles to put his gun away. With that, Charlie heads for the door. Before she reaches it, it slowly opens with a spooky creaky noise.

"Show business," says Charlie and she slowly shakes her head.

Charlie jumps off the stage and heads for the tent door; Mitchell trails behind. They meet outside. She is stumped. She doesn't know where to go next, or what to do when she gets there. Her fingers slip up to the medallion and she rubs it with her thumb.

Baker approaches.

Charlie says, "I see a poster for the bearded lady. I need to talk to her."

"You already have," says Barker.

Charlie wrinkles her brow. "What?"

"The bearded lady is Miss Clara with a wig and a fake beard. She doubles the part."

"Part?"

"Yeah, they're all really playing a part."

Charlie doesn't say a thing. She gives Mitchell's sleeve a tug and walks away, leaving Barker standing there. Mitchell dutifully follows.

"This Saturday, I want you to go to the pistol range and get checked out on your cannon. Learn how to shoot it and take it in and out of the holster."

"Oh gee, Charlie, I can't do that on Saturday."

"Why not?"

"I'm Jewish."

"Ooh, I forgot. We'll get it done after we figure this mess out. Just be a little more careful when you handle it."

Mitchell looks at his gun and nods. Charlie motions toward the wagon.

"Let's give that circus wagon another look-see."

The CSI photo van is still parked near the wagon. Charlie walks up to the back doors and slaps it with the palm of her hand. There is a muffled sound from within. The door swings open and a man sticks his head out. He squints at the bright sunlight.

"Yeah?"

Charlie holds up her badge.

"I'm Detective Chandler. This is my case. What have you found?"

"Well, I may have something, but I'm not sure. Come on in and I'll show you."

Charlie signals Mitchell to wait, and she climbs into the van.

The CSI technician takes a seat in front of a TV screen. He motions Charlie to another seat. He begins turning knobs and throwing switches. Pictures dance around on the screen.

He reaches over and puts out his hand to Charlie. "My name is Thompson, Detective. You can call me Tommy."

Charlie shakes his hand.

"Tommy for Thompson?" she asks.

"No, it's my first name. I'm Tommy Thompson."

"Okay, Tommy Thompson, what'd you find?"

"Well, it's not much. There's over ten hours of tape here. We had to do a little computer magic to find anything at all."

"So, what did you find?"

Thompson points at the screen.

"Look at this. At 0336 hours there is a slight movement of the wagon; it rocks just a little…and I think I see a small light. I think there's somebody in there, but they didn't go in the door."

"Wow, how did they get in?"

Thompson just shakes his head. "I give up."

Charlie says, "Well, thanks much, anyway. You did a great job and it was a big help." She leaves the van.

Charlie signals Mitchell to follow her as she walks toward the wagon. She has a very worried expression.

"What's wrong?"

Charlie tries to collect her thoughts.

"Go over to the big tent and ask Crozboney to come to the wagon. Remember, ask, and don't tell."

Charlie waits outside the wagon, impatiently tapping her foot. She talks to herself…out loud. Nothing intelligent, just mumbles as she reviews things in her mind.

Someone clears their throat. Charlie spins around. There stands Mitchell and Crozboney.

"Mister Crozboney, I'd like to get your professional opinion."

"The *Great* Crozboney...please."

"Okay, but that's hard to say. Can't I just call you Crozboney, or great? You can call me Charlie."

The Great Crozboney smiles. "You can call me Croz." He turns to Mitchell. "*You* can call me The Great Crozboney."

Mitchell rolls his eyes.

"Croz, if you wanted to get in that wagon without going through the door, how would you do it?"

Crozboney takes a quick look at the sides and back of the wagon, waving his arms. He looks underneath. He climbs the ladder on the end of the wagon and looks over the top.

"Well, it's actually simple to the trained eye. It reminds me of a job I had in India, we..."

Charlie interrupts. "I'd like to hear that story, but I'm on a tight schedule. Do you see how someone could get in the wagon without using the door?"

With a wave of his hand and his cape, The Great Crozboney says, "I'd use that little trap door in the floor."

"Trap door? Trap door?"

Crozboney knowingly nods.

Charlie runs up the steps, rips away the security sticker, and opens the door. She fumbles for her flashlight, but finds the light switch first.

"Trap door, where are you?"

She looks down at the oriental run.

"That's it!"

Charlie picks up the rug and drapes it over the desk. There it is! A fine line outlines the edges of a door. A large ring fitted to a door is flush with the floor and invisible under the rug. This was a piece of craftsmanship.

Charlie reaches down and gives the door a tug. It easily opens and in seconds, she's on her knees with her head sticking into the hole. She shakes her head and says, "No way." She closes the trap door, and heads out. Mitchell waits outside.

Mitchell reads Charlie's expression. "Not good, uh?"

"Not good. People must have been smaller when that wagon was built. I couldn't get through that hole."

She looks at Mitchell.

"Maybe you could fit."

Charlie returns to the wagon. She opens the trap door again and looks inside the hole. She shakes her head, closes the little hatch, and turns to the safe. She grabs the big brass handle and tugs. The thick safe door swings open. Charlie peers in. Now, the white powder is gone! The shelf has been wiped clean.

"What's going on here?"

She spots a foot stool near the roll-top desk. She pulls it over and sits down in front of the safe and stares at it.

"What's going on here?"

She rubs her thumb on the medallion.

"Something's going on."

Charlie reaches in the safe and taps the back wall with her knuckle. A hollow sound! She taps the sides of the safe. Solid. She repeats her taps of the back wall.

"It's like Croz said, a secret compartment. But how do you get it open?"

She runs her fingers around the edge of the safe wall. Nothing.

"Mitchell!" she screams.

Mitchell pops his head in the door.

"Yeah?"

"Get Crozboney again."

Mitchell takes off for the big tent in a dead run. A few minutes later, he returns with The Great Crozboney in tow. The magician is not pleased. Crozboney climbs the stairs as Mitchell waits.

"You called?" His voice reminds her of Bela Lugosi in the old Dracula movies.

Charlie stands and points at the safe.

"Hi, Croz, thanks for coming. I think there is a secret compartment in there. Can you open it?"

"Can I open it? Is the Pope Catholic?" The Great Crozboney steps forward and with a wide swing of his arm wraps his cape around the front of his body. He leans over and looks for a few seconds, and then reaches behind the safe and presses an unseen button. Inside, at the back of the safe, a panel falls forward. The secret compartment is open!

Charlie is too excited to thank Crozboney. She sticks her head in the safe and shines her flashlight around. There it is...a large plastic bag full of white powder! Cocaine! Lots of it, and more money. I'll be damned...Mitchell!"

Mitchell is standing beside her. Crozboney made his exit earlier.

"I'll be damned too," says Mitchell.

"Let's get some coffee."

"And pie?"

"Whatever you want. Fix the seal, and bring that laptop."

Carrie's Restaurant – Friday, 6/25 – 1520 hrs.

Charlie and Mitchell walk into the restaurant. They pause for a minute, just looking around. Carrie pops her head out of the little service window and gives them a "sit anywhere" wave.

They no more get settled when Carrie arrives with two cups of coffee and a piece of apple pie on her tray. "I'll be in the kitchen if you need me," she says, and walks away.

Charlie opens the computer and takes a sip of her coffee.

"How do I check my e-mail?"

Mitchell leans over and puts a finger on a key.

"Press this one. You're already on the internet, so if you have any mail, it will be there."

Charlie presses the button, and a list of her e-mail pops up astonishingly fast.

"Remarkable. How do I read them."

"Just put the little arrow over the one you want, and tap your finger twice...real fast."

"Here's one from the Narc people. Let's take a look."

She follows Mitchell's instruction.

Charlie studies the screen. "Wow!" she says, "this is wild. You know the guy in the picture?"

91

Mitchell nods.

"Well they made him. They suspect that he's a fair sized dealer. They're looking for him, and there's a warrant out. What does the paper clip mean?"

"That means something is attached to the e-mail. Double click on it."

The screen changes to reveal a standard arrest warrant form. The subject's name is Tony Alchini, a.k.a. Tony the bug.

"This is wild," mutters Charlie.

She looks all around the computer.

"How to we print a copy?"

Mitchell wrinkles his brow and bites his lower lip. "We don't. They didn't give me a printer."

"Great! Just great," complains Charlie. Then she adds, "Well if old Tony the bug comes around, we'll nab him. He doesn't know that we don't have a printer."

They sip on their coffee while Charlie studies the computer to figure out its capabilities.

"This spread sheet thing looks interesting. I think we can use it to get a handle on this case. We can list the suspects, a motive, and opportunity. Then we can eliminate some and get closer to others. What do you think?"

"How can we find a motive?"

"Motive like end of string tied in many knots; end may be in sight, but hard to unravel."

Mitchell lights up. *"Charlie Chan in Shanghai!"*

"How did you know that?"

"I went on the web."

Charlie smiles and slowly shakes her head. "Let's get busy."

Mitchell nods enthusiastically. He's excited at the prospect of doing some real detective work.

Before she can enter the first name, Mitchell's foot gently taps her under the table. She looks over at him. He has his hand up to his face, hiding, and is nodding his head toward the lunch counter.

Charlie looks over at the counter. It's the guy. It's Tony the bug!

"Take your piece out and back me up," says Charlie.

She takes her badge out of her pocket and cups it in her hand. She causally walks to the counter and sits down next to Tony. He looks over, nods and smiles. "Nice day, miss."

"It sure is! And by the way," she holds up her badge, "you're under arrest."

Tony spins around. Before he can even get his feet pointed in the right direction, he's looking down the barrel of Mitchell's cannon. He doesn't resist when Charlie pulls his arms around and slips on the cuffs. With a firm hand on his arm, she leads him outside the restaurant. It all took place so easy that the people eating and Carrie didn't even notice.

"What are we going to do with him?" asks Mitchell.

Charlie thinks for a second and looks around. "Let's stick him in the wagon until the Narcs can collect their package."

Circus Wagon – Friday, 6/25 – 1610 hrs.

They march Tony the bug into the circus wagon, and shove him in the only chair. Charlie sits on the safe, and Mitchell stands, arms crossed with his back to the door.

"Well, Mister Achini, let's talk about what you're doing here. I'm Detective Charlie Chandler, and this is Officer Mitchell Yen, my partner."

"I have rights!"

"Yes you do, and I'll have the narcotics people read those rights to you before they put you in a cage."

"Can we make a deal?" begs Tony.

"I'm a lowly cop. I can't make deals. However...if you answer my questions, cooperate, I'll tell the DA that you were a good boy. It could help. No promises, but it could help."

Tony nods his okay.

"What are you doing here?"

"I came to meet the owner...Fairall. We have business."

"What kind of business?"

"You know, business business."

"Does this business involve white powder?"

"White powder? You mean cocaine? You think I'm a druggie?" He tries to chuckle.

Charlie turns to Mitchell.

"It looks like he doesn't want to cooperate after all. Write him up for resisting arrest, drugs with the intention to deliver, and obstructing justice, anything you can think of. Toss in a few traffic things. Maybe DUI, and no license, that's a good one."

The bug's eyes grow wide. He protests, "Hey, you can't do that!"

"Well, Tony, I can. And you can take the next ten years trying to convince a judge and jury that I can't. Your call. What do you want to do?"

"Okay, Fairall and I did a little drug action. Not much, just a little. I'm not a big user. I don't deal."

"Where do you get the stuff you sell Fairall?"

The bug is puzzled. "What do you mean? I don't sell anything. I buy my stuff from Fairall. Where is he anyway? Did he squeal on me?"

"Wait a minute. You're telling me that Fairall was your supplier? I thought you were his supplier."

"Supplier? supplier? Look I got this little habit. So I do little drugs once in a while. Sometimes get some for my friends. Does that make me a bad person?"

"As a matter of fact, in my book, it does."

"I'm not a dealer. I just bought a little of the stuff for me."

"When's the last time you saw him?"

"Say, what's going on? How come you guys are in his office? You got him in the slammer?"

Charlie scratches her head. She jumps down off the safe and heads for the door.

"Watch him," she tells Mitchell, and walks out.

Charlie paces slowly under the EAT sign, trying to get a handle on things. It doesn't sound like this Tony guy is a big deal after all. He doesn't know that Fairall is dead, so he's no help.

She taps on the door. Mitchell opens it a crack and steps back. Charlie steps in. She takes her position on the safe.

"How long you been on the stuff?"

"I don't know. Maybe a couple a years. To tell you the truth, I'd love to get off. It doesn't get better, it gets worse. My wife's gone, Fairall's got all my money. Maybe I'd be better off in the slammer."

"Look," says Charlie, "I might cut you a deal after all. Here's what I can do. If you'll give me your word that you'll kick the cocaine, I'll let you go."

His eyes light up in surprise. "Let me go?"

"That's right. But you've got to turn yourself in for rehab and stay off the stuff." She thinks for a few seconds. "We'll make up a contract. You go bad and it's the slammer. Get it?"

The guy is speechless.

Charlie opens the desk drawer and roots around. "Paper," she says.

She takes out a tablet and writes a few sentences on it. She shoves the tablet in front of Tony.

"Well, what will it be?" says Charlie.

"It's a deal, lady, it's a deal. I'll go today! I'll head for Columbus and turn myself in. I'll do it now! You can count on me. You can count on me, lady."

Charlie nods to Mitchell.

He turns Tony around, and takes the handcuffs off.

"Don't worry," she waves the contract, "I will. Now get out of here. Beat it."

He's gone.

Mitchell is puzzled. "What was all that about?"

Charlie gets back up on the safe. "The guy gave us valuable information. For one thing, we know that he didn't kill Fairall; he didn't even know Fairall is dead. Secondly, he told us that Fairall was a drug dealer, not a drug user; a dealer. That's important. It could lead us to the killer. Thirdly, I'm not in the narcotics business, I'm in the murder business. If he goes astray, they'll get him. He's a minor player. Anyway, maybe the guy will make good on his contract."

"What about the warrant?"

"I don't have a warrant. Do you?"

Mitchell slowly shakes his head. He gets it, and he likes it. "Let's get back to our computer."

Carrie's Restaurant – Friday, 6/25 – 1718 hrs.

In the restaurant Charlie taps keys on the laptop while Mitchell looks on.

"Charlie?"

"Yes, Mitchell?"

"Charlie, I've been meaning to ask you something."

"Ask away."

"I'm wondering about the DNA. What are we going to do with the DNA stuff?"

Charlie thinks in silence for a few seconds.

"Mitchell, I don't know how to tell you this, but I don't have the slightest idea of what we can do with the DNA."

"Why did we collect it?"

"Good question. First, it *could* come in handy, but I'm not sure just how. DNA works better finding that someone is innocent. It's not so good for finding guilty people. Secondly, and more important, shoving a DNA swab in someone's mouth puts you in charge. It's mysterious stuff; police stuff. Besides, I couldn't think of anything else to do. Back to our list."

She starts down the list of suspects.

"I think we can rule out the fat man."

Mitchell nods in agreement.

"I don't think the snake lady could handle it."

That leaves Barker, the magician, and the dwarf.

"The dwarf is too little. He couldn't swing a two by four," volunteers Mitchell. "I think it was the magician. He's a sneaky guy. He keeps trying to change the subject."

Charlie slowly nods.

The screen door slams. "Well, hello there!" It's Barker.

Oh God, Charlie thinks, *that's all I need.*

Barker steps behind the lunch counter, opens the old soda case, and helps himself to a can of Coke. Carrie peers out of the service window. Barker gives her a hi-sign, and walks to Charlie's table. Without being asked, he sits down and takes a big swig from his can.

Charlie is not in the mood to fool with Barker. She leans back in her chair and folds her arms. Then, she springs back up and closes the computer screen so that Barker can't see. Then back to the crossed arms.

"You folks making any progress on this thing?"

Mitchell starts to say something, but Charlie stops him.

"Police work is slow. It would go faster, but we have to stop in to Dunkin' Donuts several times a day to keep going. That's where the real work happens," and she just looks at him.

Barker understands people; he knows he's not welcome here. He takes a big swig from his Coke, finishing it off, and bangs the can down on the table. "Well, I gotta get out of here. I'm seeing a lawyer today...about the will and all."

As he starts to get up, Charlie grabs his arm. "I've got a couple more questions before you go."

Barker falls back in the chair.

"How much money did Fairall owe you?"

"Owe me? He didn't owe me nothing. Remember, the place is half mine, we split the profit. After I talk with this lawyer, it's all mine."

Mitchell and Charlie just sit. Barker takes the hint. "That it?"

Charlie nods.

The screen door slams again.

Charlie watches as Barker walks past the front window. "That guy bugs me."

"I think he did it. He's the murderer alright," volunteers Mitchell.

"I thought your money was on the magician."

"Yeah, but there's something about this guy. Maybe there were two of them."

"Maybe. I've got an idea, Mitchell."

He leans forward so as not to miss a syllable.

"We didn't need the DNA, but we do need fingerprints. I think one of the three people who made it to your short list did this job. I want to get their fingerprints and run an ID check. We don't even know who these people are."

"How can we do that? We can't just walk up to people and say, 'give me your finger prints,' can we?"

"We don't need to do that," and Charlie points to Barker's Coke can. We can work with latent prints, starting with that can."

Mitchell reaches for the can.

"Whoa," says Charlie, "B and T."

"Got it, B and T."

"Now let's figure out how we can get prints from the dwarf and the magician without them knowing about it. Let's get a fresh start on Monday."

Walnut Creek Park – Monday, 6/28 – 0845 hrs.

The Big SUV coasts into the park, right past the guard shack, and stops just outside the Show Tent. Mitchell is driving, and Charlie is playing with the laptop. Charlie closes up the laptop and puts it on the floor.

"What's up?" says Mitchell.

"Fingerprints. I want as many fingerprints as we can get."

She gets out of the car and heads for the Show Tent. Mitchell follows.

They pull the flap aside and enter the big tent.

Show Tent – Monday, 6/28 – 0917 hrs.

"Where to?"

"We'll start with The Great Crozboney. I've got an idea."

Inside the tent, they head for Crozboney's apartment. Charlie pulls the giant painting aside and knocks on the door.

"Mister Crozboney, it's Detective Chandler."

The door pops open. No squeak. No lights, no music, no spooky voices. The Great Crozboney is standing there in blue jeans and t-shirt.

"What do you need this time?"

"You've been such a help, I wanted to show you a trick that my father showed me. It baffles everyone. Would you like to see it?"

Mitchell is puzzled.

The magician is trapped. This happens all the time, and he has learned to just let it happen.

"Okay, I'd love to see it. Maybe it's something I can use in my act."

"I need a deck of cards."

He steps to a table, picks up a deck of cards, and hands them to Charlie.

"Oh no, I need a new deck, unopened."

Mitchell watches in amazement and Crozboney opens a box full of decks of cards. He takes out one cellophane-wrapped package and hands it to Charlie. Charlie takes the deck and inspects it.

"This is a new deck, so the cards are in their original order," she announces.

The magician is bored. He nods and yawns.

She takes off the wrapper and breaks the seal. The magician rolls his eyes.

"Now I take out the deck," and she does.

Charlie spreads the card on the table.

"Pick a card, any card."

As if in pain, Crozboney slides one card out of the pile with a single finger. Charlie picks up the deck.

"Look at the card—don't le me see it. Now, hold it up to your forehead. Press hard and think of the card."

She holds out the deck.

"Now put the card anywhere in the deck."

With a smirk, he does.

Charlie put the cards back in the box.

"Okay," she says with a very confused expression. "Here's the good part."

Charlie keeps her puzzled look. Her head moves from one side to another.

"Hmmmmmm, let me see. This is the good part."

DAVE CROSBY

She shakes her head and puts the box of cards in her pocket.

"Darn! I can't remember that last part. I'll have to ask my dad.

She turns and starts for the door.

"What about my cards?"

"Oh, I'll get 'em back to you, after I ask my dad how to finish the trick. You'll really love it."

She leaves with Mitchell following.

When they are at a safe distance, Mitchell asks, "How are we going to get his prints?"

Charlie holds up the box of cards.

"It's in the cards, my boy, in the cards."

Mitchell nods. What a smart lady he's with.

Walking toward the tent door, Charlie talks to Mitchell over her shoulder.

"Let's see if we can work a little magic with the dwarf. What's his name, anyway?"

Mitchell checks his notes. "I don't remember. I don't think he told us."

"We can ask now," says Charlie.

Outside, Charlie heads for the Ferris wheel, which is slowly turning. Mitchell tags behind.

The midget sits on the loading platform of the wheel, reading a comic book. He looks up.

"Oh, look at this," laughs the midget. "Barbie and the gook."

"You *are* a nasty little man."

"I didn't catch your name," says Mitchell.

"I didn't throw it," the midget replies and chuckles to himself.

Charlie looks up at the wheel and then down at the dwarf.

"We want to take a ride."

Mitchell is surprised.

"I guess if I was selling donuts you'd want them free too."

"Listen, you little jerk, this is police business. Any more of your smart remarks and I'll put you in a bird cage."

"Okay, okay. Don't get in a tizzy." The dwarf reaches over and pulls on a big lever. The wheel glides to a stop.

"Get in."

Charlie steps up on the platform. She's never been on a Ferris wheel, and she doesn't know to wait until the platform is raised. She puts a foot in the footrest in the seat and as she steps in, it swings away, almost throwing her to the ground. The dwarf jumps up and steadies the seat. He helps Charlie get back in control.

"You gotta be careful, lady. This ain't a toy."

Charlie gets in the seat. The midget presses down on a lever that raises the platform and holds the seat in place. Mitchell climbs in without a problem. The dwarf closes the safety bar. He gets back in position and tugs on the big lever. The wheel starts to turn.

"Why are we doing this?" asks Mitchell.

"I don't have the slightest idea. How are we going to get that little monster's prints?"

Mitchell shrugs. "Maybe from that lever he pulls."

"Keep an eye on him; watch what he touches."

The dwarf has gone back to his comic book, and the wheel spins on. As it reaches the bottom, Charlie yells, "Okay, that's enough. We've had enough."

He acts like he didn't hear, and lets the wheel take another few turns. Finally, he stops it. He tugs on the lever to raise the platform, and as Charlie steps out, "Watch your step." He smirks.

They walk down the ramp and away from the wheel.

Charlie stops and looks back. "Do you think he did that business with the seat on purpose?"

"It'd take a lot of guts. I didn't even know the seats could swing out like that. You could get killed."

"Let's take another look at that thing."

They walk to the backside of the wheel. They stand and watch. The dwarf is engrossed in his comic book and doesn't see them. They stand looking at the passing seats.

"What are we looking for?"

"The murder weapon; we're always looking for the murder weapon."

"Murder weapon?"

Charlie stares at the passing seats.

"There's something there, but I don't know what it is. I've got a hunch; a feeling about that wheel. Fairall was killed right here; right where we're standing, right under this wheel."

"Maybe he just stood too close, and one of those seats got him. But who dragged his body over to the creek?"

"Have the dwarf stop the wheel. You stay with him. When I signal, have him move it to the next seat and stop. Get it?"

"Got it."

From where she is standing, Charlie can see that the dwarf doesn't want to cooperate with Mitchell. He's squawking and marching around in a circle. Then she gets a little thrill as she sees her partner take control. Mitchell pulls out his badge and his handcuffs and dangles them in front of the dwarf's face. Charlie can't hear what he's saying, but the wheel starts to turn.

She looks at each seat and signals Mitchell for the next one.

Nothing, she thinks. *I don't even know what I'm looking for.*

But then she sees it. One seat has a red smear on the back edge. She leans sideways to check the large painted number on the side of the seat.

She yells to Mitchell, "Bring number three around."

She sees Mitchell relay that to the midget and the wheel turns. It stops with seat number three in front of Charlie.

"Shut it down!" yells Charlie.

The dwarf hears her and walks around to the old John Deere motor and flips an old light switch, mounted on a board. The old motor slows down, coughs, and stops.

Charlie gives Mitchell a wave. Mitchell has been drinking a Coke. He hands the half-empty can to the dwarf and scampers back. The dwarf gives the can a disgusting look and tosses it away, mumbling something about gooks.

"What have you got?"

"See that stuff on the back of the seat? It's blood. I think you're looking at the murder weapon."

"Wow. How can we find out?"

Charlie slips her little Swiss Army knife out of her pocket. She steps up to the seat and runs it along the edge of the seat. She cuts off a small red sliver.

Mitchell reaches in his pocket and whips out a plastic bag.

"B and T?"

"B and T. We have to get this to the lab as soon as possible."

She looks over where the dwarf is standing and turns her back to him so that he can see her face. "Walk over there and get that Coke can. B and T it and take it back to the lab with you. The nasty little man's prints might be on there along with yours. Take the car and run it down there. Have them do the blood and run the prints too. I'll be in the restaurant."

"Keys?"

Charlie sizes up Mitchell and looks at the new SUV.

"Can you handle that thing?"

"I took care of your VW."

Charlie tosses him the keys.

He catches them, and he's off.

She walks back to the dwarf.

"I'd like to thank you for your help."

He's impressed; he actually smiles.

"That's okay, lady."

"My name is Charlie Chandler. You can call me Charlie if you'd like."

He is touched with her friendliness.

"My name's McIntosh. G. David McIntosh."

"What's the G stand for?"

"I'd rather not say."

"Well G. David McIntosh, it's been nice talking with you. Thanks for the help, and thanks for the ride. By the way, what should I call you?"

"You can call me anything but late for dinner." He laughs.

"I'll call you G. David, okay?"

He nods.

Charlie walks a safe distance and calls Mitchell on the walkie-talkie.

"This is Mitchell, over."

Charlie shakes her head and smiles. *That's Mitchell*, she thinks.

"Run the name G. David McIntosh and see what you come up with."

"Roger Wilco, and out."

Charlie takes a deep breath, shakes her head, and puts her phone away. She walks to the restaurant. She thinks to herself, *That chip and the prints could bust this thing wide open.*

Carrie's Restaurant – Monday, 6/28 – 1420 hrs.

Carrie and Charlie are sipping coffee and chatting when the SUV pulls up. "It looks like your partner's back," says Carrie.

"Better get an emergency pie and coffee ready. He hasn't eaten in half an hour."

Carrie smiles and leaves to fill the order.

Mitchell is excited. *This is getting interesting. To think I wasted a year passing out parking tickets.* He puts the computer on the table.

"The lab said they would e-mail the blood test and fingerprint results. It'll take about an hour."

Charlie checks her watch. Carrie makes it back with the pie. She sets it down in front of Mitchell, whose eyes light up. Charlie smacks her lips. "Wow, that looks good."

Carrie pulls her hand from behind her back with another piece of pie. She puts it in front of Charlie.

Charlie smiles. "Don't tell me; years in the business, right?"

"Right," says Carrie.

Charlie digs into the pie. "How do we know if we've received an e-mail? Does this thing have some kind of an alarm?"

"No, but that's a good idea. You have to turn on your e-mail program and ask for the mail."

"Okay, okay. I forgot."

Charlie pulls the little computer up close and studies the keyboard. "Now, let's see, hmmmmmm."

Mitchell, with his mouth full of pie, points to the mouse pad and mumbles some kind of instruction.

Charlie moves her finger around on the pad and nods as the arrow does what she wants. "Let's see…e-mail. Here." The laptop springs into action and things start popping up on the screen.

Mitchell takes a break from his pie and says, "Those are your e-mails. Move the pointer over the one you want and tap the mouse pad twice; real fast. That's called a double click."

"I remember now."

The words "Fingerprint ID" jump out at her. She clicks and watches.

"Wow, Mitchell, look at this. Bart Barker's name isn't Bart Barker. He's one Charles W. McIntosh." She studies the screen. "That's him, look at that mug shot. Look at the rap sheet." She pats the computer. "This thing is great."

"What about the magician? Did they check his prints?" asks Mitchell. Before Charlie can answer, he adds, "He looks mighty suspicious to me. He's tall enough to reach Fairall with a two by four, and he's a spooky guy."

"Nothing yet; the lab's still looking at that deck of cards. They say they've looked at all the cards, but they'll look again.

"Wow! Here's something on our little Ferris wheel driver. His name is Giovanni David McIntosh. Giovanni, can you imagine? He was born…wait a minute. How do I get Barker's page back up?"

Mitchell reaches over and punches a few keys. Barker's rap sheet comes up.

"Could these two guys be brothers? The dwarf and Barker were born in the same hospital. They have the same parents, and get this, the date of birth! Same parents, same date of birth. Good God, Mitchell, they really are brothers; they're twins! They've got to be twins."

"They can't be twins," exclaims Mitchell. "Barker's a normal guy; you're telling me that his twin is a dwarf?"

"Show me how to search on Google. Better still, look up 'Dwarf twins.' Try a couple of ways."

Mitchell starts his search. In just seconds, Google pays off. They study the article.

"Look at this, Charlie, one twin can be full size, and one can be a dwarf! They are Fraternal twins…two separate eggs." Mitchell nods slowly. "I didn't know that could happen."

"You're not alone. I want to get a look at Barker's apartment and go through a few things. We'll need a warrant. We should check out the dwarf's stuff too. I'll call John Spencer to get started on a warrant. When we serve it, you call for backup. He may not take it well."

Charlie pulls out her cell phone and hits the speed dial for John Spencer.

"Spencer."

"Hi, John, this is Charlie Chandler. I need a little help."

"Shoot," says John.

"I need a search warrant to search the apartment of one Bart Barker, a.k.a. Charles W. McIntosh, and a G. David McIntosh, both at the Walnut Creek Amusement Park address. I'm looking for drugs and money, and information about Fairall's murder. There's probable cause all over the place."

"Okay. Send Mitchell over in a while, and I'll have it."

Mitchell should be on your door step in about five seconds."

"Okay, see ya."

"See ya."

Mitchell gets the idea and starts to leave.

"Hold on," says Charlie. "They won't have anything for a couple of hours. John has to run down a judge and sell him on the idea."

Mitchell settles back and checks out the menu again. Charlie gets up to leave.

"I'll be in the wagon until I hear from John." She knows that John Spencer knows how to work the system and that there is nothing for her to do just now.

Circus Wagon – Monday, 6/28 – 1520 hrs.

Charlie breaks the seal on the door and puts in the key. She notices that the seals are starting to pile up, making it harder and harder to turn the key. She steps in and flicks on the lights. Everything looks normal.

While she's waiting, she decides to take another look in that safe.

She grabs the foot stool and pulls it over in front of the safe and digs in.

Fairall must have kept every piece of paper he ever had, she thinks.

Receipts, old letters, photos, how-to-do articles, and on and on. "This guy didn't have a very exciting life," she says out loud to no one.

The she finds something very interesting...Fairall's last Will and Testament. Two copies. One dated about five years ago, one dated last week!

Her cell phone rings. "Chandler," she answers.

"Hi, Charlie, John. I've got your paperwork. I can't make it down there, the boss is having a fit. Can you send Mitchell up?"

"Great! He'll be there in a flash, thanks. I'll let you know what happens."

Charlie steps out of the wagon and walks to the window of the restaurant. Mitchell is eating pie just inside the window. She taps on the window to get his attention and waves for him to come out.

He hurries with his last bite of pie and heads for the door.

"What's up?"

"Run over to headquarters and get the warrants from John."

"I'm gone."

Charlie searches her pockets for the keys to the SUV.

Mitchell holds them up. "I forgot to give these back to you," he says sheepishly

Charlie smiles and points to the main gate. "Go!"

Charlie turns and walks to the wooden stairs. She sits down to wait.

In a matter of minutes, the SUV pulls up and Mitchell hops out. He's waving a neatly folder sheet of paper.

"Got it. I called for backup."

"Great. Let me read that thing to make sure we're on firm ground."

"Got some bad news," says Mitchell.

"What?"

"The lab couldn't find the magician's prints on the cards. They said they checked every single card—twice—and nothing. Then, they counted the cards, and one was missing. Was the magician's card the three of diamonds?"

Charlie burns. She realizes that the magician got the best of her. Somehow, he made her believe that he had put the card back in the deck. "I don't have the slightest idea what that card was, that son of a...He tricked me! He didn't even put the card back in the deck, he tricked me!" Then she laughs. "Serves me right. Admitting failure like drinking bitter tea." *Charlie Chan in Egypt.*

Mitchell jots that down in his notebook, but is afraid to say anything. He just stands by for instructions.

"We have to wait till our backup gets here."

Mitchell nods.

"There they are now; coming in the gate!"

Charlie looks up. "That's not one of ours, that's a sheriff car."

They watch as the car pulls up close and comes to a stop. Two uniformed deputies get out of the car. One heads toward Charlie; the other opens the back door and drags out two teenage boys, both wearing handcuffs.

The first officer, a sergeant, taps the bill of his hat. "Are you Miss Chandler?"

"Detective Chandler." Charlie nods.

"Well, we've got the culprits who took a shot at you."

Charlie looks at the kids. She's puzzled.

"Them? I don't get it."

"We caught these two kids playing on the other side of the creek. They had a twenty-two pistol, and were taking shots at everything and anything. We checked the tent here and found bullet holes in most of those big posters. I think that the bullet that hit you traveled through at least three layers of canvas, so it lost most of its stuff before it hit you. That canvas, those posters saved your life, miss."

Charlie's hand flies up to grab her medallion. "I don't know what to say, except thank you very, very much."

She looks at the boys. "What happens to them?"

"Well, they're in deep shhh…huh, big, big trouble. There's more than the shooting, so I think the State will be feeding them for some time. Don't worry; they won't be back on the street for about four or five years."

The deputy taps the brim of his cap, turns and gets back in the cruiser. The kids, heads down in shame, are shoved back in the car.

Charlie and Mitchell just stand, watching them drive away. There's nothing to say.

Charlie starts toward the restaurant. "Let's have a coffee and talk this thing over. I have an idea."

Carrie's Restaurant – Monday, 6/28 – 1645 hrs.

They walk in the restaurant and take a seat at a back table. Charlie opens the laptop, and loads her spread sheet.

"Let's go over this. We can rule out the fat man and Wilma. I don't think the snake lady could do it, but like you said, she could hire somebody. The magician loved Fairall, so he wouldn't do it. That leaves Barker, a.k.a. McIntosh, and his little twin. Maybe Barker figured out what Fairall was doing, and wanted to get in on the drug business. Then there's RT. I know he has something going with the dwarf."

Mitchell listens to very word. "Who is this RT character, anyway?"

"I don't know about RT. Maybe the Narcs can help there. Remember that sliver of wood that I cut from the Ferris wheel seat?"

Mitchell nods. "Yeah?"

"Well, I got an e-mail from the lab that says it's Fairall's blood. That means that the seat *was* the murder weapon!"

"How could you bonk someone over the head with a seat? They must weigh a hundred pounds. Maybe more."

"I don't know, Mitchell. It's been a long day."

At that moment a black and white curser pulls up outside the restaurant and two uniformed officers get out. They look around to get their bearings. Charlie spots them and heads for the door. Outside, she

109

holds up her badge and identifies herself to the two officers. "I'm Detective Chandler; this is my partner, Mitchell Yen."

One officer, a black sergeant, introduces himself and his white partner. "I'm O'Reilly, that's Jackson. You need help?"

"Yeah," Charlie says, pulling out the warrants. "We're going to do a little search, and I'd appreciate it if you guys could stand by."

"You expect trouble?" asks O'Reilly.

"I don't know, but I'd like a show of force. Nobody is going to misbehave with you guys standing there."

With that, the group heads for the show tent.

Charlie pulls aside the flap and steps inside with the others close behind. She feels a tinge of concern when the shooting thing replays in her mind. She yells out, "Barker! You home?"

They walk the length of the tent and Charlie starts up the wooden stairs. The others follow. Unseen by Charlie, several paintings move slightly as some of the performers peek out to see what's going on.

Reaching in behind the giant painting of the Elephant Man, she bangs on Barker's door. "Barker, you in there? We need to talk."

Charlie can hear activity inside the apartment and steps close to the door. Officer O'Reilly, gun drawn, gently pulls her back and to one side. He doesn't speak.

The door opens and there stands Barker wearing a bathrobe. His hair is wet, and he obviously just stepped out of the shower.

"What's going on?" he asks.

"I want to look around your place, Mister Barker...or should I say McIntosh?" she says, holding up the paper. "We've got a warrant."

Barker's head drops. "Okay, come on in, but you're wasting your time."

"We'll talk about that later."

"What are you looking for?"

"Oh, I think you know. How about drugs and money for starters? Does that ring a bell?"

Barker looks at the two officers. "Search on, you won't find that kind of stuff here. I don't have anything to do with drugs, and you know that I don't have any money."

The apartment is the same size as the others so it doesn't take much time. Charlie is surprised that Barker is so neat and organized. She and Mitchell go through everything; everything, and find exactly nothing. What a disappointment.

Unwilling to show defeat, Charlie says, "Okay for now; we'll check next door."

Charlie leads the way to the dwarf's apartment. His apartment door is behind the Cat Lady's painting. Charlie knocks.

"David! Are you in there?"

"Hell No," a voice yells, "I'm down here. What the hell do you want? What is this, a raid?"

Charlie turns around to see G. David McIntosh standing on the ground below her.

"I've got a warrant, David. We want to look at your stuff."

The dwarf scampers up the stairs and directly to his door. He gives the uniformed officers a very nasty look, and unlocks the door.

Charlie steps into the dwarf's apartment. It's like a doll house, and she feels like a giant. The place is very well furnished, all in scaled down furniture. It's really quite nice, not what she expected at all.

"What are you looking for?" asks the dwarf.

"Drugs and money," replies Charlie.

The dwarf shakes his head. "Do whatever you need to do and get out of here...please."

It takes less time to search the dwarf's apartment than Barker's. The place is clean. Clean! *What's going on here?* Charlie thinks. *Are these people so smart that they can fool us, or are they really clean?*

"Do you want me to show you out?" says the dwarf in as nasty a tone as he can muster up.

Charlie looks down at him. "We'll be leaving now, but I have my eye on you, little man."

He watches them all leave, and slams the door behind them.

Outside, Charlie and Mitchell walk the officers back to their car. "This is what you call your basically weird place," says the sergeant.

"You got it," replies Charlie. "But, if you're looking for a place to eat," she motions over her shoulder, "you can't beat Carrie's place. Great food and she likes cops."

O'Reilly smiles, and with a little salute, climbs back in the cruiser. Without ceremony, they are up the hill, out the gate, and gone, leaving Charlie and Mitchell standing outside the restaurant.

"Can you imagine? The McIntosh brothers were clean!" says Mitchell.

"Maybe too clean," replies Charlie.

"I've got to take a break and think about things. Let's knock off for today and see if we can wrap this thing up tomorrow. I think we've found all the physical evidence. Go ahead and take down the tape so they can open." Mitchell does, and the big black SUV cruises out of the park carrying two exhausted cops.

Police Headquarters – Tuesday, 6/29 – 0810 hrs.

Charlie finds a side-chair so Mitchell can sit by her tiny desk. Charlie's desk is right out of the nineteen thirties. It's actually half a desk. The top opens and a spring loaded shelf that once held a typewriter pops up. The typewriter is long gone, and Charlie hasn't opened the thing since it scared the wits out of her the first time she did it. She has a tablet in front of her.

"Here's the way I see it," she says, moving the tablet so Mitchell can see. "Remember how the seat on the Ferris wheel almost dumped me?"

"Yeah?"

"Keep that thought in mind. Here's the way I see it happening. Fairall and Barker are under the wheel arguing about the drug business, right there where we found the blood. I think Barker either wanted in, or wanted to take over. The park is closed and the wheel is not turning. Fairall is standing with his back to the wheel. The argument gets hot. The dwarf—G. David—sees his brother getting the worst of the argument and jumps up on a seat. The seat swings out and takes the back off Fairall's head."

Mitchell is awestruck. "Wow. So who's the murderer, Barker or his twin?"

"That's up to the courts to decide."

"Let's go get them!"

"Not so fast, it's just my theory. We have to collect evidence that puts Barker under the wheel with Fairall. I'm sure there's plenty of stuff on the dwarf—he works there so it would be useless. Barker is a different story."

"We have the DNA."

"I don't think that's going to help us."

"What are we going to do now?"

"I'd like to look at the photos of Fairall's body, and see exactly what CSI found. We know that somebody moved the body; maybe they left something behind." She lays a little Charlie Chan on the subject. "Murder always bring something to crime scene; always take something away."

"Cool," Mitchell chuckles, "Charlie Chan?"

Charlie nods and walks to Wilson's office with Mitchell tagging behind. Wilson is on the phone when they arrive, so they stand outside his glass enclosed cubicle. When his conversation is over, he waves them in.

"Detective Chandler! Great to see you!" Wilson stands up and shakes hands with Charlie. He points to a chair for Charlie, and gives Mitchell a nod.

"How can I help you, Miss Chandler?"

"It's Charlie, remember?" she jokes. "I'm still out there at the amusement park and I'm running out of leads. I'd like to see the photos you folks took, and the report that describes your findings."

"You got it. No problem."

Wilson picks up the phone and presses the "Call" button. "Shirley, would you bring in the Walnut Creek Amusement Park folder?"

Only a few seconds pass before a very attractive young black woman walks in holding a large packet. She hands it to Wilson, and stands silent.

"Charlie, this is my secretary Shirley. She also happens to be my baby daughter," he says with a proud smile. "Shirley just graduated from State, and I convinced her that she could learn a lot working here. It's just a summer job. Shirley, this is Detective Charlie Chandler and Officer Yen."

Shirley smiles and shakes Charlie's hand. "I'm pleased to meet you, Miss Chandler; Officer Yen."

Wilson stands and hands the folder to Charlie. "You'll have to look at that stuff here; I can't let it out of the office. You can use the conference room." He points to a door across the hall. "Would you like coffee?"

Charlie takes the package. "Coffee would be great," and she starts for the conference room door.

Shirley bursts into a big smile. "I'll get your coffee."

Charlie opens the package and spreads the material out on the big conference table. "Where to start?" she mumbles. Mitchell joins in the search.

She pokes around, not knowing what she's looking for. There are several eight by ten black and white photos and a few in full color. She separates them from the rest of the material and sits down to give them a closer look.

"Would you ask Shirley if they have a magnifying glass?"

Mitchell springs to action and Charlie pulls the photographs closer. A few minutes pass and she realizes that Mitchell hasn't returned with the magnifying glass. She gets up and walks to the door. She looks up and down the hall. No Mitchell. She steps out and walks toward Wilson's office, and finds the problem. There is Mitchell, leaning on the wall, talking with Shirley. He looks like a school boy. Charlie clears her throat. A shocked Mitchell looks up and immediately heads for Charlie, magnifying glass in hand.

Charlie returns to the photographs.

Using the magnifying glass, Charlie studies the photographs; Mitchell sits quietly. Suddenly, Charlie gets up and leaves Mitchell at the table. She mumbles something, but Mitchell can't understand. He decides just to wait it out.

Charlie appears at Wilson's door. She knocks lightly on the door frame.

He looks up and smiles. "Need something?"

She puts the photos on his desk. "Can you get a close-up of this area?"

"Not a problem," says Wilson. "It will only take a few minutes. Would you like a disk with copies of these photographs? You can view them on your computer."

"That would be great, but I'm not the best when it comes to computers, so if you could blow these spots up, it would be a big help."

"Give me a couple of minutes."

Charlie returns to the table.

"What did you find?" asks Mitchell.

"I'm not sure if I found anything. Wilson is making a couple of enlargements. He's going to give us a disk with the pictures on it. Do you know how to work those on our laptop?"

"Oh, yeah," says Mitchell. "There is one problem...we don't have a printer."

"Well, let's see how it works out and if we need a printer, we can ask John."

Just then, Shirley walks in with the pictures. "They made extra copies of the original for you and here is the blow-up." She hands the photos to Charlie. "Oh yeah, here's the disk too."

Charlie looks at the disk, raises one eyebrow, and hands it to Mitchell. "Let's go."

Charlie waves as she passes Wilson's office. He's on the phone, so she just blows him a kiss in thanks. She turns to Shirley. "Good luck on your job, Shirley."

Shirley says, "Thanks, I'll need all the luck I can get."

Mitchell can hardly stand it! What did she find? Finally, he asks. "What did you find out? Anything good?"

"A couple of things, but I'm not sure what they mean. Fairall had some strange marks on his chest; two small circles, and a small spot of white powder on his lapel."

"Cocaine?"

I don't know. I've got to look at the lab's chemical analysis to find out what it is."

The rest of the ride back to the park was in silence—Mitchell paying attention to his driving, Charlie studying the CSI report.

The SUV pulls into the park and Charlie tells Mitchell, "Pull in there by the Show Tent."

Mitchell does, and they get out.

"What's up?" asks Mitchell.

"I've got a couple of questions for Wilma."

"The fat guy's Wilma?"

"You know another one?" She didn't feel good about that remark, but she had something on her mind and didn't have time for small talk.

Show Tent – Tuesday, 6/29 – 1122 hrs.

Leading the way, Charlie charges into the tent and walks to the fat man's apartment...she knocks. "Wilma? Can I talk to you?"

Wilma opens the door and gives Charlie a big smile. She holds her index finger up to her lips. "Shhhhhh, Pete's asleep." She squeezes out the door and quietly closes it behind her.

"What do you need?" asks Wilma.

"What kind of powder to you use?" asks Charlie.

"I don't use face powder."

"Bath powder?"

"Yeah, I use bath power. Nothing fancy, I think it's called Shower and Bath, or Bath and Shower. I get it at the market. Why?"

"Tell me, Wilma, why would Fairall have your powder on his suit coat?"

Wilma is shocked; she doesn't know what to say. There is a long silence. Charlie waits.

"I don't like to talk about the dead," says Wilma.

"This is important, Wilma. A man has been murdered. Now, how could your bath powder find its way to Fairall's coat?"

Wilma frets. In a very weak voice, she tells Charlie, "Bill made a pass at me." She quickly looks around. "I don't want Pete to find out, he'd be furious."

"Tell me about it. Don't worry about Pete."

"There's nothing to tell. I had to take some papers down to the office. Bill was there and I think he had a couple of drinks or something; he grabbed me and tried to kiss me. I got loose and came home. That's it. That's the only time it happened. I think he was drunk."

"Okay, Wilma, don't worry about it; if there's anything else, I'll let you know."

Charlie and Mitchell walk back to the SUV and drive it to the circus wagon.

"How did you know about the powder?"

"It was in the CSI report; bath powder on his coat. It was one of the spots that I saw on the photographs. There was a fair sized spot and two circles. I don't know what made the circles.

"How did you know it was Wilma?"

"I smelled it when we were in the apartment."

"Wow," says Mitchell in a very low, quiet voice. "You can do that?" Then he points his index finger in the air. "Any powder that kill flea is good powder."

Charlie stops dead. "Where'd you get that?"

Mitchell smiles. He's very pound of himself. "Charlie Chan, *The Wax Museum.*"

"He wasn't talking about bath powder, he was... Well, never mind. Watch the movie again."

Mitchell is worried that he has done something wrong—and he has.

Charlie doesn't say anything. They start toward the restaurant.

Carrie's Restaurant – Tuesday, 6/29 – 1305 hrs.

They enter the restaurant and head directly for their table in the back corner. The laptop comes out.

"Let's see if we can eliminate some more people," says Charlie.

Mitchell checks his watch. "Can we eat lunch?"

No answer.

They study the spreadsheet. Charlie runs the pointer up and down the screen as if she's waiting for lightning to strike when she hits the right spot. She's not getting any signals.

"Maybe that fat guy hired someone," says Mitchell.

"Maybe."

Mitchell quickly nudges Charlie. She looks at him and he nods toward the counter.

Charlie looks. It's RT! She quickly huddles with Mitchell.

"I want to get his prints. Are you wearing a t-shirt?" He nods.

"Take your jacket and shirt off. You're going to be the busboy. See that glass he's drinking out of? You play busboy, fill up a new glass with water, put it in front of him and grab that glass he's using. Say as little as possible. Act like you don't speak English. Dump the glass and head for the kitchen. Go out the back door and go to the SUV. I'll join you there with your coat. Remember, just touch the very top of the glass; we don't need your prints.

Mitch sets out on his mission as Charlie watches. He gives an academy award performance, smiling while he puts down a fresh glass of water. He has obviously pleased the big black man. He smiles and utters a few sounds that might be taken for Chinese, and disappears into the kitchen.

Charlie gets up to leave just as RT turns around. He spots her and waves.

"Hi, little girl," he yells, "come on over."

She's trapped. She leaves Mitchell's coat and shirt hanging where he left them and slowly walks to the counter. "Hi, RT, what's up?"

RT spins on his stool to face her. She can't help but think about how big this man is.

"You back already? Have you eaten yet?"

"Yeah, I just finished," she lies. "I've got to get over to my mother's house; she's not feeling well," she lies again.

"I can run you over there; wait till I finish my sandwich."

"No, I can't. I've got a ride. Gotta go. I'll talk to you later. I have your number." She heads for the door, forcing herself not to look back. Mitchell is in the SUV, motor running. Charlie gets in.

"Where's my coat?"

"Oh!"

Mitchell's upset. "I'm going back."

"Oh no," pleads Charlie.

Mitchell jumps out of the van and heads for the back door of the restaurant, and disappears inside. Charlie can see RT sitting at the counter, and is praying for Mitchell to get back. She sees the swinging kitchen doors open and Mitchell steps out. He puts his hands together in a prayer-like gesture and says something. Of course, Charlie can't hear. Then she watches as Mitchell runs to the table, picks up his jacket shirt, and heads for the front door. In seconds, he's out of the restaurant and in the van. She slips it in gear and they are off. Charlie's pulse is working over time.

"Where's the glass?" she asks.

Mitchell points his thumb over his shoulder, telling Charlie to look on the back seat.

"Let's hit the lab," says Charlie as they clear the main gate.

Crime Lab – Tuesday, 6/29 – 1610 hrs.

Wilson is always more than happy to show people around his wonderful lab and show off all the CSI equipment. She handed him the glass, all wrapped up in a napkin.

"We need to get prints off that and run them. Can you do it?"

"That's what we do best." He takes the glass, examines it and hands to a young woman in a white lab coat.

"Let's get some coffee while that's going on. With any luck, we'll have an ID in twenty-five or thirty minutes."

The trio sits at the big conference table and Shirley dutifully brings coffee.

"I think we could have used your help yesterday," says Charlie. "We searched two apartments for drugs, money, or anything else, and came up empty. It was a dry well. I think both of these guys are dealing cocaine, but we didn't find a spec."

"Did you use a dog?" Wilson asks. "You can't rely on people; the dealers are too clever. I always use a dog."

Silence as Charlie realizes her mistake.

"You know, you've got something there." She turns to Mitchell.

"When we finish here, let's get a K-9 unit and go over to the McIntosh brothers' apartments. I think our warrants are still good, but I'll have to check."

Mitchell nods.

Shirley sticks her head in the door. "They're ready," she says.

Wilson leads the way to the fingerprint lab. "What have we got?" he says to the technician.

"Well, I think I've got a surprise. ID'd two people on the drinking glass. One is a cop named Mitchell Yen. The other is a cop named Richard T. Booker." She hands Charlie the report." That's it!" she adds.

Charlie is dumbstruck. RT is a cop. Is he a good cop, undercover, or is he a dirty cop?

"Let's go see a man about a dog," says Mitchell.

Charlie starts laughing out loud. She can't stop.

Finally, Charlie winds down and Mitchell asks what was so funny.

"See a man about a dog. That's what my dad used to say when he was going to the restroom." And she started laughing again.

She puts out her hand to Wilson; he takes it. "Many, many thanks. You guys were a big help."

On the way out she calls John Spencer.

"Spencer," he answers.

"Hi, John, this is Charlie. How do I get a K-9 drug dog?"

"You can get a dog down at Pet Palace. You want the dog, or do you want a cop and a dog."

"Very funny," says Charlie, just a little ticked off. "I need a cop with a drug dog."

Spencer realizes that his joke didn't go over. "Where are you now?"

"I'm just down the hall, outside CSI."

"You take off for the park; I'll have a unit meet you there."

"Tell them to come to the big tent; the show tent."

Show Tent – Tuesday, 6/29 – 1728 hrs.

Charlie and Mitchell sit inside the SUV waiting for the K-9 unit. Mitchell breaks the silence.

"Did you look at the Fun House?"

"Yeah, the so-called Fun House is an empty shell. Barker told me they sold off all the equipment, so it's not much fun anymore."

As she speaks, Charlie thinks she sees one of the canvas walls of the Fun House move. She looks closely…nothing. She continues her conversation.

"I wonder if this place ever made any legal money. It looks to me like Fairall kept the place going with his little drug business. That's all tax free."

"Tax free?"

"All money is tax free if the government doesn't know anything about it."

"Oh, I get it."

The K-9 unit arrives. A single officer and a German Shepard. Charlie sizes up the uniform. *About forty, white, balding, at two ten, he's a little overweight for his five eight form.* She thinks if he could lose the mustache and goatee beard, he'd look sharp in his uniform. He gets out of the cruiser and leaves the dog in the back seat, peering out the window at Charlie.

Charlie puts her badge in her breast pocket and approaches. Seeing this, Mitchell gets his badge in his pocket in a flash. Charlie puts out her hand. "Detective Chandler. Charlie Chandler," she says. "This is my partner, Officer Mitchell Yen." Mitchell steps forward and shakes hands with the K-9 officer.

"My name is Schott. John Schott. People call me Bus."

Charlie feels good about the guy. "Okay, Bus, we need your help."

The cop looks around. "I didn't know this carnival was in town. When did they get here?"

"About 1934," says Charlie.

"I didn't even know it was here. What's the problem? How can I help you guys?"

"We've got a warrant to search a couple of apartments in that tent for drugs and money. We already looked once, but we need your dog. We'd like to take a second look."

The officer walks to his cruiser, opens the door, and takes the Shepard out on a short leash.

Charlie thinks how vicious the dog looks. She's not too sure how she should behave, but decides to stand back and let the pair do their job.

"Where do we go?" asks the cop.

"Follow me," says Charlie, leading the way.

She bangs on Barker's door. "Mister Barker, you in there?"

In just seconds, Barker opens the door. "What? Again?"

"We just want to take one more little peek. This time with a dog."

Barker looks down at the dog and his eyes open wide. He's terrified. He quickly stands back from the door. "A dog? Well, okay, I guess," he stutters.

The officer and his dog step into the apartment and do their stuff. It only takes about three minutes and they are back at the door.

"It's clean," says the cop.

"Clean?"

"Clean. What's next?"

Charlie gives a brief wave to Barker and he disappears behind his door. She moves to the dwarf's door and bangs. No answer. She tries the door. It's unlocked. She pushes open the door and motions the officer to go in.

The dog leads the officer around the room and back to the door. They all step outside, and Charlie closes the door.

"Clean," says the cop.

"Okay, I guess that does it. Thanks for you help. Can I pet your dog?"

The K-9 officer gives his German Shepard a jerk on the leash and walks to Charlie. Cautiously she reaches down. The dog looks up at her.

"He's a baby doll," says the officer, and they head for the exit.

"Clean," says Charlie, shaking her head in disappointment.

Mitchell just stands by.

"Come on," says Charlie. They walk back to the SVU, climb in. They sit in silence.

"What was that?" Charlie says, excitedly.

"What was what?"

"I think I saw that flap on the Fun House move. I think somebody's in there."

No sooner are those words out of her mouth when a large hound dog walks out of the tent. He sniffs around, pees on the flap, and jogs away.

"A dog," says Charlie.

The silence resumes.

"Let's knock off and get a fresh start in the morning."

She starts the SUV and starts pulling away when she notices something in the rearview mirror. That tent flap on the Fun House moved! But she decides it's just the wind, another dog, or her nerves.

The SUV clears the gate headed for Police Headquarters.

The Fun House – Tuesday, 6/29 – 2200 hrs.

Charlie tried to watch TV, tried to get to sleep, but she couldn't get that tent flap out of her mind. *I know I saw it move*, she tells herself. Dressed in jeans, t-shirt, cuffs, and gun, Charlie drives back to the park.

It's late and the park is quiet. She pulls the SUV up to the Fun House, cuts the lights and kills the engine, and sits. Certain that nobody has seen her arrive, flashlight in hand she steps out of the SUV and gently closes the door—just enough to turn off the overhead light, but careful not to make any noise. She stands quiet, letting her eyes adjust to the darkness. It's spooky, and she hears all sorts of strange sounds coming from Walnut Creek. Dogs bark in the distance.

Charlie takes a deep breath, turns her light on, and aims it at the tent flap. Slowly, cautiously, she steps toward the entrance to the Fun House. Remembering that the hound dog had peed on the flap, she carefully pulls it open using only her index finger and thumb. She slips inside and flashes the light around in a quick search.

Charlie can feel her heart pounding. Slowly, she moves around the building, searching, for what she doesn't know. The place is full of old broken machinery—wheels—belts—boxes. Everything is covered with a heavy layer of gray dust. *This stuff must have been here forever,* she thinks.

A sound! She turns off her light and stands there, listening. For what seems like an eternity, the only sound now is her breathing and rapid heart beat. Then, something touches her leg! She gasps, but stands still. All sorts of pictures flash through her mind. A giant snake. A bear. A wild bobcat. She feels warmth from the thing leaning on her and hears heavy breathing. She's about to strike out with the heavy flashlight, but with all her courage, she turns on the light and looks down. The hound dog is smiling up at her.

Weak in the knees, it takes a few seconds for her to recover. Timidly, she reaches down and pats the dog on the head. "Good boy," she says. She's made a friend.

Charlie re-starts her search, her new best friend at her side. Every time she touches something to get a closer look, a large black nose appears to check it out. Then she notices something that is clean—dust free! A picture! A picture of a large apple with lettering around it. She takes a closer look. It's a wooden box with a colorful label on the end; an apple crate. The crate is partly covered with a large piece of dirty canvas. Charlie pulls the canvas aside, but doesn't move the crate. She peers into the box. Money! The box is full of bills. She takes out a bill to examine it. No dust. *This must be the money from the safe,* she thinks.

Charlie carefully replaces the bill and pulls the canvas back over the box exactly the way it was. She turns and heads for the door, the dog following close behind. She stops at the SUV to gather her thoughts. *I'll leave it here for now; maybe I can find out who's hiding all that loot. They've got to come back. No, wait! Maybe I can get fingerprints from one of the bills,* she thinks. Charlie hurries back to the apple crate, peels back the canvas and carefully removes a bill—a fifty. Holding the bill in the palm of her hand, she once again heads for the exit. The hound dog is close behind.

Charlie opens the door of the SUV, and before she can climb in, the hound dog springs up into the front seat and waits, looking out the window like he belongs there. Charlie feels sorry for him, and is not certain what to do. Finally, she points to the ground and tells the dog, "Come on, you be a good boy and get out. I'll bring you something special tomorrow." The dog sits still, looking out the front window. "Did you hear me? Now you get out before I call the pound."

The dog's ears pop up and he immediately leave the car. His sad eyes watch as Charlie gets in. She starts the engine, slams the door and heads out. In the mirror she can see the expression on the big dog, watching her leave. She feels bad, and starts thinking about what she can do to help the dog. She stops at the top of the hill and looks back. Poor baby. As she watches, the dog sniffs around Barker's old Plymouth. He spends a lot of time on the trunk, going around the edges. He sits down and looks in Charlie's direction. Then he walks to the Fun House, and disappears behind the flap.

Talking to herself, Charlie says, "I'll bet the poor baby is hungry. He thinks he can find something in that old car. I'll have to bring something for him to eat tomorrow. What do dogs eat?"

Police Headquarters – Wednesday, 6/30 – 0800 hrs.

Charlie sits alone at her desk, lost in thought. Mitchell shows up with a fresh cup of coffee.

"Morning, Charlie."

"Hi, Mitchell. How are you doing today?"

He holds up his coffee in a salute. "What's the plan?" Handing her a business envelope he says, "They gave this to me up front. Mail for you."

"Mail?" She opens the envelope, pulls out a letter-sized piece of paper. She reads it and smiles. "It's a letter from our fried Tony. He says he's in rehab, and doing well. He's going to make it."

"That's great, really great."

"He wants to know if I will give him a recommendation when he gets out and starts looking for a job."

"What are you going to do?"

"Guess." She folds the letter and puts it back in the envelope.

Let's get down to business. Something has been bugging me. Last night, I went to the park very late to have a look at the Fun House. This is Top Secret, so keep quiet about it. I found an apple crate full of cash."

Mitchell's eyes show his surprise. "Last night? Cash?" he whispers.

Charlie continues. "I also found a stray dog that makes me wonder if there's something in the trunk of that old car."

"Was it a drug dog?"

"I don't know. I think it's just a dog dog. But it sure was interested in that old car. Think about it. If you wanted to hide something, the trunk of an old car would be a good place."

Mitchell gives a weak smile. "Maybe we should ask The Great Crozboney."

She gives him a look.

"Yeah, I guess that wouldn't be a good idea," he says timidly.

She holds out a large, clear, plastic envelop with the fifty dollar bill in side.

"Run this down to Wilson and see if he can get any prints," she says.

"Done!" replies Mitchell and he heads for the lab.

In a few minutes, Mitchell is back. "He says it's hard to do, but sometimes they get lucky. He'll let us know later. Shirley is going to the movies with me Friday."

Charlie pops up and starts to leave. "That's great. I hope you two get along. Come on; let's take a run out to the park. I want to check out this trunk business. First, I have to talk with John. Then I want to stop by the seven-eleven and get some dog food."

"Dog food?" he mumbles.

He tags along with Charlie as she heads for John's desk. John is there with his feet on the typewriter shelf and his hands clasped behind his neck. He's out on Lake Erie again. He looks so peaceful that Charlie hates to bother him.

"John? John, I've got a question."

John pops out of his daydream, but he missed what Charlie said. "Hi, Charlie, what's going on?"

"I have a question."

"Shoot."

"That warrant we got yesterday. Can I search an old car on the property?"

"That warrant will let you search anywhere in that park. What are you looking for?"

"Well, I'm not sure, but I've got a hunch about an old car."

"You're safe. If you have any trouble, give me a call."

With that, Charlie and Mitchell leave and head for Walnut Creek Amusement Park by the way of Seven-Eleven. When they arrive at the park, Charlie heads the SUV straight for the Show Tent. She parks, and they go in.

Show Tent – Wednesday, 6/30 – 0945 hrs.

"Barker? Are you in there, Mister Barker."

Wilma sticks her head out behind the fat man's poster. "He's not here, Detective. I think he went to Columbus to see a lawyer."

"Okay, Wilma, thanks. I'll see him later." She leaves; Mitchell follows. They are headed for the old car.

The Old Plymouth – Wednesday, 6/30 – 0950 hrs.

When they arrive, the hound dog is waiting. He's delighted to see Charlie and runs to meet her.

"Watch out for the dog," warns Mitchell. "He's big enough to do some damage."

Charlie opens the plastic envelope of dog food and puts it out on the ground. It immediately disappears and the dog is looking for more. She opens the second and last envelop. This time, she asks the dog to sit. He does. She asks him to shake. He does. She gives him the food.

"You're a good boy," she says, rubbing his head. "Sometimes I wish I could keep a dog."

She turns to the tasks at hand. "You know anything about old cars, Mitchell?"

Mitchell looks a little ashamed. "Not much…" he says. Then he reconsiders, "Nothing at all."

Charlie walks around the car looking for the best way to get in. "See if the doors are locked, Mitchell."

Mitchell tries the passenger side. Locked! He walks around to the driver's side. It's not locked, and looking at Charlie, he pulls it open.

"Pop the trunk," says Charlie.

Mitchell searches around and under the dashboard, but can't find a lever to open the trunk. "What years is this?" asks Mitchell.

"Barker said it was a forty-one."

"Nineteen forty one? I don't think they popped trunks in those days. My uncle had an old car and I know he had to have a key to open the trunk. He lost his key one time, and had to get a locksmith."

"Try the trunk lid," instructs Charlie.

Mitchell tries. It's locked.

"Only one thing to do…" says Charlie, "…like your uncle, we need a locksmith. Let's go to the wagon and use the yellow pages. Maybe there's one close by."

They leave the old car and drive to the circus wagon. It turns out that there is a locksmith about three or four miles from the park. Charlie talks with him on the phone. The words "Police business" had a remarkable effect. He agrees to come over. ASAP.

"What now?" asked Mitchell.

"We go to the car and wait."

The locksmith arrives just minutes after Charlie's call. Charlie files him away in her data bank. *White, fifty-five or sixty. Five seven, a hundred and fifty pounds, bald, blue slacks and white shirt, black shoes.*

Charlie puts out her hand as he approaches. She pulls out her badge and puts it in her breast pocket. Mitchell quickly does the same.

"I'm Detective Chandler. I have a warrant to search this car and the trunk is locked. Can you open it?"

The locksmith takes one looks and says, "It's a snap. You want a key made?"

"I just want in to take a look. One thing I have to ask. When you open it, please walk away without looking inside. For your own good, you don't want to know what's in there. It's police business. Just unlock it and stand back. Got it?"

The guy is worried. "I guess so…"

"No guessing. You unlock it and stand back. I don't want you to see what's in that trunk. By not looking, you'll save yourself a lot of grief."

"I'll do what you say, lady."

"One more thing. Keep it under your hat that you did this job. It'll help you get jobs from the police department."

Now, the guy is really worried. Mouth hanging open, he nods.

"Okay, open it up."

The locksmith bends down to look at the handle. He nods and open takes a small packet of lock picks from his shirt pocket. It just seconds, he turns the handle and the trunk lid moves. He stops right there.

"What's the damage?" asks Charlie.

"Fifty bucks."

Charlie reaches in her pocket and takes out three twenties. "Here, keep the change, you did a great job. Now, I'll ask you to leave so that we can get on with our search."

Without a word the guy gives a little salute and gets in his van. He starts it up and drives off.

Charlie runs to the Plymouth and pulls up the trunk lid. The trunk is full of plastic bundles of white powder. Cocaine! Bags, and bags, and bags of cocaine!

Mitchell looks around to see if anyone is watching. "Cocaine?" he asks.

"I think so, but we better be sure. You have any plastic bags?"

Mitchell reaches in his side pocket and pulls out the last of his baggies. "Last one," he says.

"Forget it."

Charlie runs back to the SUV to find a pair of rubber gloves. She slips them on and returns to the Plymouth. There, she picks up one of the bundles, and lowers the trunk lid so as not to lock it again. She takes the package to the SUV.

"I want to test this stuff. Do you know how to use that test kit?"

"We did it at the academy, but I've never done it for real."

"Well, there's a first time for everything."

Charlie watched as Mitchell nervously operated the tiny kit.

Working out of the back of the big van, Charlie uses her Swiss Army knife to make a very small incision in the package. She takes out a small amount of the white powder on the knife blade and puts it in the test tube.

"If it turns blue, it's cocaine."

Almost before Mitchell can finish his sentence, the liquid in the vile turns blue.

"Cocaine! That trunk is full of cocaine. There must be ten million dollars worth of the stuff in there! What are we going to do?" asks Mitchell.

"We got a first-aid kit in this thing?"

Mitchell points to a white box with a green cross. "We've got enough stuff to do brain surgery."

Charlie laughs. "That's a clever remark, Mitchell. See if you can find a small band-aid in there."

Mitchell roots around in the first aid case and finds the band-aids. He hands one to her and watches. Charlie removes the tape from its wrapper. She takes a quick look around and walks to the old car. Mitchell tags along.

One more quick look around, and Charlie sticks the band-aid on the trunk over the crack. "If anyone opens that trunk, we'll know about it."

Mitchell smiles; he's impressed with his partner's ingenuity. "What do we do now?"

"First, we're going to run this over to the lab and see if they can find prints. Then we have to get the Narc people involved in this. It's more than we can handle. Then we go to Carrie's and eat lunch."

They climb in the SUV and head off for headquarters.

CSI Lab – Wednesday, 6/30 – 1130 hrs.

Wilson examines the package and shakes his head. "It's hard to get prints off this material, plus, if we get something it might be some farm worker in Columbia. We'll give it a shot and send whatever we find in an e-mail. How does that sound?"

"That's great!" says Charlie. "I don't know what we'd do without you guys."

Wilson smiles, gives a little wave, and heads to the lab.

"Wait," calls Charlie.

Wilson spins around and faces Charlie.

"We have to get that package to narcotics when you finish with it. I'll let them know you have it, and we'll go from there."

Wilson waves his understanding and continues his journey.

"What now?" asks Mitchell.

"I'm going to get something to eat. How about you? Want lunch?"

Mitchell breaks into a big grin.

"You want to go to Carrie's, or find a new place?"

"Carrie's!" says Mitchell. "I love that cheeseburger."

Carrie's Restaurant – Wednesday, 6/30 – 1246 hrs.

They head for what has become their regular table. Carrie's head pops out of the service window and she waves. The place is busy.

Charlie studies the menu, but Mitchell squirms in his seat and looks around for Carrie.

Charlie chuckles. "You hungry?"

He just nods and his eyes follow Carrie as she walks to their table.

"How are my favorite detectives doing today?"

Mitchell looks up. "I'll have the cheeseburger-fries-apple pie-milk shake," he says as one word.

"He's hungry," says Charlie. "How are you today, Carrie?"

"I'm always great when we're busy...and we're busy. What'll you have, Charlie?"

"I'm going to stick with that wonderful grilled cheese sandwich and diet Coke."

Carrie turns. "Coming up," she says and walks back to her kitchen.

Charlie slides the salt shaker back and forth from one hand to the other, like a hockey puck. She's thinking.

"You know what, Mitchell?"

He doesn't answer, but gives her his undivided attention.

"We should have had this case solved and the bad guy locked up by now."

Mitchell doesn't know what to say.

Charlie slips back into her thought. *What am I doing wrong? What would Dad do? I knew I couldn't do it. Why did I get into this mess? What's next?*

Lunch comes and they eat. No conversation, they just eat.

Charlie pushes her plate away and takes another drink of her diet Coke.

"You got the laptop?"

Mitchell points to a vacant chair and mumbles. His mouth is full of hamburger.

Charlie reaches over and gets the little computer and sets it up in front of her. She has to search around to find the on/off switch. Mitchell points it out.

She waits while the computer does all its start up stuff and then clicks the e-mail icon. Something from Wilson! She opens the e-mail.

Charlie: 1. We were able to find several clear prints on the package. Two of them don't show up in the database, so I think they are the farm workers or mules that I told you about. The other print belongs to one Charlie McIntosh, a.k.a. Bart Barker.
2. The prints on the bill belong to G. David McIntosh.
Hope this helps. Wilson

Charlie rocks back in her chair and utters a low, "Wow."

Mitchell shrugs his shoulder.

Charlie spins the laptop around so he can read the screen. His eyes register his surprise.

Carrie stops by with the check.

"How was that meal?" she asks.

"Couldn't be better," answers Charlie. "We have to get goin' now. What's the damage?"

"Well, " says Carrie, "it seems that I overcharged you the last time. Don't know how it happened. Must be getting old. You don't owe anything today. We're square."

Charlie smiles. "Well, that's the first good news I've heard today."

She reaches in her pocket and finds a five dollar bill. As they get up to leave, she tosses the bill on the table. "Let's hit the road, partner."

"Where to?"

"I want to talk to the Narc people about all that stuff we found. That part is their show, and we've got to tie them in.

Narcotics Department Office – Wednesday, 6/30 – 1518 hrs.

It's been a while since Charlie had any dealings with the narcotics people, so she doesn't know exactly who to see. The office is much like the pit, only half the size. It too has a corner office. *We'll start at the top*, Charlie thinks.

The corner office is a glass enclosed cubicle like Fadler's. The office door is closed; a woman is at the desk. The sign on the door says, *Susan M. Paschall. Director*

Charlie taps on the glass.

The woman looks up from her work and motions Charlie in.

Charlie signals Mitchell to wait, and she opens the door and walks into the office. The woman stands to meet her, and extends her hand. They shake hands.

"Susan Paschall."

"Hi, I'm Detective Charlie Chandler, homicide. I need to talk with you about some drugs."

Susan's eyes lit up. "I'm always happy to talk about drugs. What's the story?"

Charlie opens her witness data bank. *Female, white, dyed auburn hair, pushing sixty, slim, maybe one ten, five feet six, wedding ring.*

She waves Charlie to a side chair.

"I'm working on a homicide over at the Walnut Creek Amusement Park. In the course of my investigation, I keep running into drugs. I didn't think I had enough to get you people involved until I discovered an old car with a trunk full of bundles of cocaine."

"Are you sure it's cocaine?"

"We opened one package and tested it...it's cocaine. That package is down at the crime lab. They were able to get some prints."

"Goodness, you have been a busy little bee," says Susan.

"The problem is that I'm not certain just yet if the drugs and the murder are connected. If we do this wrong, we could end up with a trunk full of drugs, but no dealer and no murder. Know what I mean?"

"I think we can work things out. Let me assign someone to help you. Just a minute, please." She gets up and leave the office and leaves Charlie sitting in the chair. Mitchell is looking in the glass door. She motions him that it's okay, just wait.

Susan must have been gone fifteen minutes and when she returns, Charlie almost falls off her chair. RT is walking behind Susan! *What's this all about?* she asks herself.

Susan introduces RT. "This is agent Booker. He's been working undercover. He told me about meeting you. He's the guy to help you, but remember, he's under cover and it would be very dangerous for his identity to get out."

Charlie waves for Mitchell to come in. "My partner has to be tied into this," she says.

RT shakes hands with Charlie. "Well, it's really nice to meet the real you, Miss Chandler."

"Please call me Charlie, and this is Mitchell Yen, my partner."

"Hi, Mitchell, I'll stick with the RT business, if you don't mind."

Charlie feels panic coming on. Here she is with people who know what they're doing and she doesn't have a clue about what to do next.

"It's late now," says Susan, "why don't you two get together in the morning and figure out the best approach."

"Great! But I do have one question I'd like to ask RT," says Charlie.

RT steps forward. "Shoot."

"What's the connection with Miller and Fairall? Is Miller Fairall's supplier?"

RT smiles. "No, I don't think so. Miller is interested in developing that property, but I was talking with him about building a house."

"No drugs?"

She motions for Mitchell to follow. Under her breath she says, "Saved by the bell."

"Oh!" exclaims Susan, "wait a minute. I know I've heard that name before. Charlie Chandler. Are you related to the gentleman who worked here years ago?"

"Yes, that was my dad."

"They used to call him Charlie Chan. Have they started on you yet?"

"No, but I wouldn't mind. Charlie Chan had a lot to offer."

Susan smiles and nods.

Charlie looks at RT. "Well, I'll see you in the morning. Oh eight hundred?"

"Oh eight hundred," answers RT.

Charlie walks back to her desk in a daze. Things are starting to move fast. Maybe too fast.

Chinatown – Wednesday, 6/30 – 19:14 hrs.

The Chinese buffet is located on the edge of the town's small Chinatown. San Francisco, it's not. About a half a block of typical novelty shops, jewelers, souvenirs shops with the usual stuff.

Charlie and Mom walk along arm in arm, enjoying the windows. Suddenly, Charlie stops and grabs Mom's arm. "Let's go in this jeweler shop; there's something I want to check on."

No sooner had they entered the shop than an old Chinese man, in full Mandarin costume, appeared, arms crossed, hands up his sleeves. "Welcome," he says and bows slightly. "How may I help you?"

Charlie steps up to the counter, slips her medallion off her neck and holds it up to the man to see."

"Can you tell me what this says?" Charlie asks.

The old man swings a light with a huge magnifying light around to examine the medal.

"Oh," he says, "this very powerful coin. Very powerful."

Charlie is excited. "What does it say?" Pointing to the large letters, she asks, "What does this mean?"

The old man holds the medallion so Charlie can see. "This mean...courage, this mean...knowledge, this mean...wisdom. Very powerful." He hands it back to Charlie.

"Courage, Knowledge, and Wisdom," she says in a dreamy voice. She presses the chain and medallion to her breast, smiles, and releases a sentimental sigh. Glassy-eyed, she turns and heads for the door. Mom follows along.

As they reach the door, the Chinese man calls out, "You need more?"

Charlie turns to look back.

The man holds up at least a dozen chains and medallions exactly like Charlie's. "You want more? I have plenty more. You want?"

Charlie pops back into reality. She looks at the man and looks back at Mom. Slowly, she smiles and turns back to the man. "Thanks, but I'll just keep this one, it works."

With that they head off to the buffet.

"You know what, Mom?"

"What, Charlie?

"I halfway believed that this medallion had some magic power. I know it's silly, but when it saved my life, I knew it gave me power."

Mom doesn't answer, and they start their attack on the buffet.

Later, Mom turns the table on Charlie.

"You know what, Charlie?"

She gets the joke. "No. What, Mom?"

"Your medallion thing reminds me of when you were just a little kid. Your favorite story was about the duckling that couldn't swim."

"I remember. The little duckling couldn't swim because he was afraid, so his mother gave him a stick and told him it was a sky hook and that it would hold him up—keep him from sinking. So when he was holding the stick..." She stops and smiles. "I get it. I had a fear of failing and the medallion was my sky hook. My problem is that I have been chasing Charlie Chan!"

Mom smiles and nods. They finish their meal and open their fortune cookies.

Mom reads hers. "Mine says, 'You will be a successful person.' That's nice."

Charlie breaks her cookie and pulls out the message. "Mine says, 'HELP! I'm trapped in a Chinese cookie factory.'"

"Charlie!"

"You know, Mom; I think I've got this Amusement Park thing figured out. I know exactly what to do. When we get back to the house, I have to sit down and write out a plan. Tonight!"

Police Headquarters – Thursday, 7/01 – 0800 hrs.

Charlie is only a few minutes late for her meeting with RT. Being undercover, he's not well known in the narcotics department. When she finds him, he's sitting at a tiny desk just like hers. Because he's so large, it makes the desk look even smaller.

"We found all these bricks of cocaine in the trunk of an old car," Charlie starts.

"I noticed that old Plymouth. Had one like it when I was a kid. I hate to tell you that I didn't think about looking in the trunk. What made you do it?"

"You won't believe it, but a stray dog was pointing to the trunk!"

RT shakes his head. "Strange...by the way, bricks are a kilo of marijuana. Cocaine has a whole bunch of tags."

"Okay, these were bags."

"No," says RT, "bags are heroin."

Charlie is exasperated. "Well, whatever they are, there's a bunch of drugs in the trunk of that car. I put a band-aid on the trunk so you can tell if it's been opened."

"Okay, we'll keep an eye on it without tipping off the owner. When you're ready to make an arrest, let us know."

"You'll need a locksmith to get in the trunk."

RT smiles. "We have methods. Don't worry, we'll get in the trunk."

Charlie stands up; she feels good about this meeting. "Great, I've gotta go," and she leaves.

Back at her desk, Charlie works on her plan. Mitchell arrives, coffee in hand. He slips into the side chair by Charlie's desk and carefully puts the paper coffee in a safe spot. Charlie looks up from the yellow pad and smiles. "Good morning, partner."

Mitchell smiles and nods. He's munching on a chocolate chip cookie.

"This is going to be a very good day, Mitchell. A very good day."

"What's up?"

"Today, we're going to put this whole case in a box, wrap it up, put a bow on it and drop it on Fadler's desk." She smiles and looks down at the pad.

"What's going on?" asks Mitchell.

"You'll see in a minute. We've got a lot to do. I want you to drive over to the park and personally visit each of the performers and tell them that there will be a meeting in the Show Tent at 1400 hours, and that it's in their best interest to attend."

"What do I say when they ask what it's about?"

"Just tell them I said to be there. After the meeting gets started, I want you to get that apple crate from the Fun House, and hold on to it until I give you the signal to bring it to me."

"Where is the crate?"

"Go into the Fun House. Turn right and walk down the aisle. Maybe thirty, forty feet in, look to your right. Look under that piece of canvas. It was in plain sight when I first saw it. It's got a big label on the end of the box with a picture of an apple. You shouldn't have any trouble, but if you do, beep me on the walkie-talkie."

Mitchell nods, but he's not certain how he's going to find the apple crate.

"I've got to run around here and get people lined up. When you finish handing out your invitations, meet me back here and we'll have lunch—on me."

"Where do I get the invitations?"

"I didn't mean physical invitations. You're going to invite them to attend."

Mitchell slowly nods, then takes the last sip of coffee and tosses the cup in the waste can. "See you later," he says.

Charlie watches him go and can't help wondering. *Oh well,* she thinks. *Oh ye without faith. Mitchell will come through.*

She gathers up her yellow pad and a few loose sheets and walks to the stairs. *Boy,* she thinks, *I've got to get a desk on the main floor...and a real desk.* She starts on her mission.

First stop is with Susan Paschall, the Narc lady. Susan waves her into the office.

"Good morning, Charlie, good to see you," and she offers her hand.

"Good morning, Miss Paschall."

"Susan."

"Okay, Susan, I need your help."

"You've got it. What do you need?"

"I'm going to wrap up the Walnut Creek Amusement Park case today, and I need one of your people standing by to make an arrest and take possession of a lot of white powder in the trunk of an old car. RT can help; he knows the park. I think it's his case."

"RT is undercover. I'll send a uniformed officer. Don't worry, RT will know about it and get credit. We just have to protect him. Now, what do we do?"

"I'm going to assemble all of the people involved in the Show Tent at 1400 hours. I plan to place the drug dealer under arrest, but your guy will have to take over."

"That sounds simple enough. It may take more than one officer. I'll have a team show up a little before two o'clock."

"Great. This is so exciting. It's been wonderful working with you, Susan, and I hope we'll be working on other cases."

"Can I tell my grandchildren that I worked with the famous Charlie Chan?"

"I've got a long way to go before you can call me Charlie Chan, but go ahead and tell them."

Charlie leaves and walks to Fadler's office. She stops at John Spencer's desk. She can see the Chief sitting at his desk. John looks up.

"Hi, Charlie, this is an unexpected surprise. What's up?" He motions her to the side chair.

"I'm going to wind up the amusement park case today and make the arrests. I would like you and the chief to be there when I do it. I want to show him first-hand what a dumb broad can do. Any chance of him being there?"

"I think he said brainy broad, not dumb broad. No matter, I'll sure be there. I'll have to play it by ear as far as Fadler goes. He may go for it, or he may have a conniption, you never know. What's the deal, anyway?"

"Well, I'm going to have all the performers assemble in the Show Tent, and make the arrest in front of them. They are all affected, so they have a right to know what's going on. We're talking about big-time drugs, grand larceny, and murder. It should be quite a show."

"Isn't that a little unusual? It's kinda like the old black and white movies."

"It's exactly like the old movies. That's why I'm doing it."

"Two P.M.?"

"I'll be there."

Show Tent – Thursday, 7/01 – 1400 hrs.

Charlie assembles all the players in a semi-circle. Wilma, the tattooed lady; miss Clara, The Snake Lady; The Great Crozboney; Barker the barker; G. David McIntosh the dwarf, Fred Doer, the maintenance man, and Carrie the restaurant owner. The fat man has his door propped open so he can hear. Uniformed backup officers are standing by. Before Charlie starts, Chief Fadler and John Spencer walk in. Charlie notices that they have arrived, but doesn't react.

She walks to Barker's side. He doesn't resist when she pulls his hands together behind him. He's confused. "What's this?" She slips on the cuffs

140

Charlie steps in front of him. "Mister Barker, or should I say Mister McIntosh, you're under arrest for possession of a controlled substance, namely a car trunk full of cocaine—with intent to deliver. The gentlemen in the blue police uniforms over there will read your rights to you. Have a nice day." She nods to the officer Susan sent, and he walks forward to take charge of Barker.

"You know about the old car?" she asks the officer.

"I've got people out there right now."

Charlie turns to address the group. "I doubt if any of you knew it, but Mister Barker, a.k.a. Charles McIntosh, was hiding cocaine in that old Plymouth convertible. This stuff is right from the grower. Barker is a big-time dealer. Big time dealer."

Once again, the group exchanges surprised glances and comments.

She signals Mitchell to grab the dwarf, but before he can, the dwarf takes off running. He makes about a three yard run before Mitchell nails him with a flying tackle. He goes down hard and is roaring mad. Charlie is surprised to see this aggressive side of Mitchell. She nods her approval.

"Get off me, you big slant-eyed gook!" screams the dwarf.

Mitchell ignores the remark. He starts to slip on the handcuffs but has a problem. The dwarf's arms are too short to reach together behind his back. He gives Charlie a "what do I do now?" look. She reaches around her back and takes out her set of cuffs and tosses them to Mitchell. Hooking the two sets of handcuff together in a chain does the job. G. David McIntosh is secure.

She then motions to Mitchell to get the apple crate. He nods and leaves.

"Perhaps you folks noticed the apple crate full of money. It came out of the Fun House, where Mister McIntosh stashed it. He's been collecting it for some time. He assembled all this cash by sneaking into the Circus Wagon through a trap door and stealing from Fairall's safe. Lucky for Mister McIntosh here, the safe wouldn't lock, so he just helped himself to a little cash each night."

Mitchell returns with the apple crate and sets it down by the dwarf.

Charlie walks to the dwarf. "Giovanni David McIntosh, you are under arrest for grand theft. All that money you have been stealing during your nightly visits to the circus wagon belonged to Fairall, so now I guess it belongs to the person or persons mentioned in Mister Fairall's will. That's for the courts to figure out. Right now it's evidence."

Charlie turns to the dwarf. "Like your brother, the police officer will read you your rights just before he tosses you in that black and white car out there. I have reserved a cell without a trap door."

The dwarf lets loose with every swear-word he's ever heard.

There is a rumble of conversation among the performers. Charlie hears the word "brothers" and decides an explanation is in order.

"That's right, folks; Bart Barker and the dwarf are brothers— twins. Barker's real name is Charles McIntosh. G. David and Charles are fraternal twins."

The rumble of conversation starts again as the performers discuss what they have heard.

"It happens. They are what's known as Fraternal twins—two eggs—one daddy. They could have been born at different times, but they were born at the same time, so that makes them twins. Now we get to the murder of William Fairall. The action that brought me to this lovely park.

"I doubt if you folks knew it, but Fairall was a drug dealer. Big time drug dealer. I don't know if he and Barker were partners or competitors. I think that will come out later, during the trail."

Performers mumble their surprise.

Carrie Sheppard walks to Charlie and gives her a hug. "I'm so proud to have known you, Charlie. Don't forget me. I'd love for you and Mitchell to visit the restaurant from time to time."

Charlie wipes a tear from her eye and continues. "I guess that both Barker and his twin *brother*, G. David, wanted in on the action."

More mumbling.

"That would be an obvious motive for murder. They are a couple of bad guys, but they didn't kill Fairall."

"Actually, Fairall's death may have been an accident or maybe it was manslaughter at the most. We'll have to wait for the Medical Examiner to look at what I'm about to tell you and decide. Then, the wheels of justice will turn. I don't have anything to do with that decision. My job here ends when I place the person I believe was responsible for Fairall's death under arrest.

With that, Charlie walks to the USS Kearsarge. Fred stands by his cart, holding the handle. In a very formal tone, she says, "Fred Doer, I'm placing you under arrest for the murder of William Fairall." She steps forward and gently puts her hand on Fred shoulder. He looks at her with sad eyes. "I'd like you to go over to those police officers so they can take you downtown. You'll be okay."

A confused Fred Doer sadly complies. About halfway to where the officers are standing, Fred turns to Charlie. "It was an accident, you know. I didn't mean to hurt him, but he wouldn't get me the parts I need to keep things running. I guess I got angry and shoved the Kearsarge at him. He fell backward and the seat caught him. I didn't mean anything. I'm very sorry. I'm also very sorry for letting the air out of your tires. I guess I wanted to show off the Kearsarge." With that he looks at the ground and resumes his walk. While the officers are putting the cuffs on Fred, he speaks to Charlie again. "Will you look after the Kearsarge for me? I'd hate for anything to happen to her."

Before she can answer, The Great Crozboney steps forward. "I'll take care of it, Fred; I'll keep it in perfect shape for you."

Tears flow down his cheeks as the officer leads Fred from the big tent.

Charlie faces her audience. "Fairall died from what we call blunt force trauma to his head. Fred didn't hit him, but Fred caused him to be hit. Here's what I think happened: The night Fairall was killed, Fred was working on the Ferris wheel. Fairall stopped by to see how the work was going. The wheel was slowly turning when Fairall joined Fred.

"Fred asked about some parts he had ordered. Fairall told him he wasn't going to get them, and Fred reached his boiling point. In a moment of anger, he shoved his cart, the USS Kearsarge over there, into Fairall, knocking him backward and into one of the Ferris wheel seats as it passed by. Fairall was hit on the head, and that was the end of him. Fred, in a complete state of panic, moved the body to the creek, where it was found."

John Spencer is enthralled with Charlie's analysis. "How did you know it was the maintenance guy?" he asked.

"His cart, my visit to the morgue, and the crime scene photos I got from CSI. If you examine the photos, you'll see two circles, or rings on Fairall's chest. I noticed bruises on Fairall's cheek at the morgue, but it didn't register until I saw those photos. If you look at the Kearsarge, you'll notice two pipes sticking out of the front where Fred told us he planned to put halogen lights. When Fred pushed the cart at Fairall, those pipes hit him in the chest and knocked him into the path of the seat."

"What about us?" asks the magician. "What are we going to do?" All the performers nod and exchange worried expressions.

Charlie reaches in her inside breast pocket and pulls out the folded piece of paper she took from the safe. She opens it up and holds it in front of her.

"You'll be happy to know that Fairall wasn't completely a bad guy; he loved this show, and he loved you people. I think the reason he got into the drug business was to support his habit—this circus you call an amusement park. What I have here is the last Will of a Mister William Fairall. It was dated about two weeks ago, so it's probably his last will. I found it in Fairall's safe."

The performers mumble and gather closer together.

Charlie continues. "Fairall left everything, except the restaurant, to…" Everyone leans forward, and Charlie can't help but think of the academy awards: "the award goes to…" She continues. "To a trust to be divided equally among each of you. He lists—by name—the fat man—Wilma—the snake lady—the magician—Barker, and G. David. The courts will have to decide if the McIntosh brothers will get anything. They probably will because they didn't have anything to do with his death. I don't think it looks good for poor old Fred."

Everyone is obviously relieved and pleased as they exchange words.

"So what do we do now?" asks Wilma, the ex-tattoo lady.

"Well," smiles Charlie, "it looks like Fairall trusted you to manage things. I'm not a lawyer, but it looks to me like he wanted you to be the administrator."

With that she hands the document to Wilma. Then she picks up the apple box full of money and puts that on the stage. "This money will have to go to the evidence locker until the business with G. David is settled. I'm sure your lawyer will know what to do."

The uniformed narcotics officer walks in the tent and calls out to Charlie. "Detective Chandler!"

Charlie walks to meet him. He's waving a small piece of paper, a note from Susan Paschall. He taps the brim of his hat and hands Charlie the note. She opens it and reads it, then bursts into a big smile.

"What's up?" asks Mitchell.

"This is a note from Susan Paschall—the Narc lady. She says that the dog that helped us is a drug dog that walked away from a San Francisco drug officer. Somehow, he worked his way to Ohio and to the Walnut Creek Amusement Park. Isn't that grand?"

"San Francisco? How long was he missing?" asks Mitchell.

Charlie looks at the note and nods. "San Francisco. Two years! He's been out there looking for help for two years. That's quite a dog." For a moment she considers asking Susan if she can have the dog. Naw, that won't work.

"You ready?"

He nods.

"Let's go...I'll drive."

As they leave the tent, they hear the sound of applause from the performers. Chief Fadler and John Spencer are clapping louder than anyone else.

John slowly shakes his head and says, "Boy, life is gonna be an adventure with that lady."

And the town's newest detective team departs.

Printed in the United States
80028LV00002B/35